AN UNEXPECTED FROST

BOOKS IN THE TUCKER SERIES

Tucker's Way
An Unexpected Frost
April's Rain
March On

AN UNEXPECTED FROST

David Johnson

LAKE UNION
PUBLISHING

This book is a work of fiction. Names, characters, businesses, organizations, places, events, and incidents either are the product of the author's imagination or are used fictitiously. Any resemblance to actual persons, living or dead, or locales is entirely coincidental.

An Unexpected Frost is a new release of a previously published edition. This new edition has been updated and edited.

Text copyright © 2014 David Johnson

Published by Lake Union Publishing, Seattle
www.apub.com

Amazon, the Amazon logo, and Lake Union Publishing are trademarks of Amazon.com, Inc., or its affiliates.

ISBN-13: 9781477827055
ISBN-10: 1477827056

Cover design by Jason Blackburn

Library of Congress Control Number: 2014943977
Printed in the United States of America

This book is dedicated to all the loyal Tucker fans. Your enthusiasm for the Tucker books has been an inspiration to me. Many people are not able to get past Tucker's crusty, prickly exterior and are turned off by the story before it gets started. That you all feel such strong positive emotions for Tucker shows you've learned the important lesson of not judging people too quickly or judging a book by its cover.

CHAPTER ONE

Slapping March on the back of his head, Tucker barks, "I tol'ja t' warsh th' back o' yore neck, didn't I? It's as dark as yore hair. Come here."

Grabbing his shoulder, Tucker pulls him to her. His feet fight for traction on the gravel road.

Tucker pulls a red bandanna out of her back pocket and spits on it several times. Pinning March's head against her side with her thick arm, she begins scrubbing his neck with her free hand.

"Ow!" March yells. "That hurts. Not so hard!" Like a mouse under a cat's paw, he squirms.

"Hold still," Tucker growls. "If'n y' done what I tol'ja, y' wouldn't have t' have me do it fer y'. Miss Ella invited us t' 'er house fer a git 'gether. An' you're not gonna look like some kinda orphan child."

Satisfied with her work, Tucker releases her quarry.

March dances a few feet away, gingerly touching the back of his neck. He scowls at Tucker as he stuffs his shirttail back into his jeans. "Ever since you got them new eyeglasses you see dirt everywhere."

Self-consciously adjusting her glasses, Tucker says, "That's 'cause I couldn't see it b'fore. Miss Ella bought 'em fer me. First new pair I've had 'n ten years. I didn't know how bad m' eyes was gittin'."

They walk a few more steps and March says, "What's a git 'gether?"

"Darned if I know," Tucker replies. "Miss Ella's always throwin' some kinda new word at me. I guess we'll see when we git there."

A few moments later, March stops abruptly and cocks his head to one side. "Hear that?" he says smiling.

Pausing beside him, Tucker cups her hand behind her ear. A faint *plinka, planka* reaches her ear. She mirrors March's smile.

"It's Smiley Carter playing the banjo!" March says excitedly.

Tucker nods her head. "I b'lieve you're right."

When they walk past the large lilac bush at the corner of Ella's front yard, they get a clear view of the porch.

Sitting on the porch rail, head bent over the guitar cradled in his lap, is Shady Green. His hand is strumming up and down like pistons in a racing engine as he tries to keep pace with the quick tempo of the song.

Smiley Carter is standing with his banjo hanging from his neck. The fingers of his right hand are orchestrating a perfect imitation of Earl Scruggs's three-finger roll, while his left hand slides up and down the neck deftly forming chords. Sitting cross-legged at his feet, looking up in admiration, is August.

Leaning back slightly in a straight-back chair is Ella. Her Autoharp lies on her lap like a sleeping baby. Her easy strumming fills the air with rich-textured chords.

Standing in the middle of the group is April, blond hair shimmering. Her eyes are closed as she sings the final phrase of "Worried Man Blues"—"I'm worried now, but I won't be worried long."

All three accompanists end on the same stroke.

"Wooo weeee," exclaims Shady Green. "Tha's my-ee fy, my-ee fy!"

Slapping the porch with both hands, August yells, "You said it, Shady Green. That is mighty fine!"

"April," Smiley Carter says, "your voice gets stronger ev'ry time I hears you sing. An' it's as smooth as honey. I'm telling you, God done give you a gift, child. Treat it precious."

Embarrassed, April drops her head.

"What do you say?" Ella prompts her.

Lifting her head ever so slightly, April looks through her eyelashes at Smiley Carter and says, "Thank you."

Carter smiles broadly. "You are welcome, child."

Leaning over to lay her Autoharp on the porch, Ella says, "I'm going to get us some water." When she stands, she sees Tucker and March walking toward them.

"Tucker!" she exclaims. "And March! There you are. Come on up here and join us."

When March doesn't break into a run toward the porch as she expects him to, Tucker looks down at him. He glowers at her. His shoulders are pulled so high they nearly touch his ears.

"What's got in t' you?" Tucker asks. "Y' look like a tomcat ready fer a fight."

"Nothing," March shoots back at her and shoves his hands deep into his pockets.

"Then straighten up yore face," Tucker says. "We's here t' have a good time."

As they approach the group on the porch, August stands up and meets them. He smiles as he stands in front of Tucker.

"Look at how that boy's growed," Smiley Carter says. "He's as tall as you, Tucker."

"Yeah," August says to Tucker. "I can really look at you eye to eye now, especially since you got them new glasses." Patting his oversized Afro, he adds, "And my 'fro makes me look taller than you."

Folding her arms across her chest, Tucker gives him her best stony expression. "Must be all that food y' eatin' over at Smiley's. Y' stays over there more'n y' stays with me. Besides, you're fourteen years old now. 'Bout time y' started growin'." Leaning forward to look more closely at his hair, she adds, "Is that a rabbit I see hidin' in that bush?"

Raucous laughter rings through the group.

It's then that Tucker notices April standing quietly beside her. Reaching down and picking her up, Tucker says, "And here's m' beautiful April. Purty as always."

April reaches her arms around Tucker's thick neck and buries her face between Tucker's neck and shoulder. April takes in the familiar aroma of Tucker that clings to her clothes—the smoke from her woodstove, the sweet odor of her chewing tobacco, the lingering smell of this morning's bacon, and the faint smell of soap that indicates Tucker took the unusual step of washing up before coming to Ella's.

They stand entwined for several moments. Silence falls on the others as they take in the beauty of this intimate scene.

Ella takes out a tissue and dabs at the corners of her eyes.

When April and Tucker release their hold on each other, Tucker sets the girl on the ground.

The rural mail carrier passes by in a cloud of dust. Everyone facing the road throws up their hands in a friendly greeting.

Tucker turns her attention to the porch. "Didn't know there was a music show goin' on down here. Ya'll chargin' admission?"

Carter slides a cane-bottom ladder-back chair toward Tucker with his foot. "Hush up ol' woman, and have a set'tee with us. I'm still waiting to hear you sing a song. I've heard rumors you ain't half bad."

Ignoring Carter, Tucker looks at Ella and says, "Who gave an invite to that dark bag o' hot air?" Then, quick as a frog catching a willow fly with its tongue, Tucker turns to Carter and says, "An' th' next time y' call me an 'ol' woman,' I'm gonna call on th' spirit o' Mama Mattie t' put a hex on y'."

Carter's smile fades as quickly as a mouse skittering into its hole. "Don't be speakin' foolish talk about the dead—'specially Mama Mattie. She visits me in my dreams sometimes."

Ella watches for Carter's familiar smile to reappear. When it doesn't, she motions Tucker toward the empty chair. "Sit down, sit down. I'm so glad you decided to join us." Noticing that March hasn't stepped on the porch yet, she continues, "And, March, how would you like some lemonade?"

Still frowning, March slowly steps toward Ella. "I'd like some," he says.

Ella quickly gets out of her chair. She takes two steps and then suddenly reaches out to grasp one of the front porch posts, closing her eyes.

Tucker's brow furrows. In a voice tinged with concern, she says, "Ella, are y' all right?"

After a few seconds, Ella opens her eyes and relinquishes her hold on the post. "Well," she says, looking at the worried expressions on everyone's faces, "I guess I got up too quickly. I got a little swimmy-headed. I'm fine now."

Ella disappears into the house and quickly returns with two glasses of lemonade. Holding one toward March, she says, "Here's one for you, March." Turning, she hands the other to Tucker. "And one for Tucker."

March quickly begins draining his glass.

Watching him, Tucker says, "Didn' y' fergit somethin', boy?"

March cuts his eyes toward Tucker as he continues to drink. Slowly, he lowers the glass from his lips. He mumbles something and then looks at Ella and says aloud, "Thank you, Miss Ella."

Shady Green speaks up. "'ucker, ooo ice shooo isss purrry."

As usual, it takes everyone a few beats to translate Shady's speech-impaired words into something intelligible.

"I agree with you," Carter says. "Tucker does have some pretty eyes. I didn't remember what color they was; it's been so long since I seen 'em. What color would you call 'em, Miss Ella?"

Smiling, Ella says, "Tucker's eyes are magical. Their color ranges from green to gray to blue depending on the color of the sky. Some people call it hazel."

Tucker tilts her head up and grips her glasses with the thumb and index finger of each hand. She sniffs loudly. "I think they make me look like I got culture." Unable to contain herself, she laughs out loud.

Laughter runs through the group like a needle and thread, sewing their spirits together.

As the laughter dies, they hear the high-pitched sound of squealing brakes from the road. They turn to see the mail carrier's car stop. The dust cloud from his trail down the road catches up and engulfs his vehicle. Once the dust passes, he opens his door. Carrying a clipboard, he approaches Ella's porch.

"Hey, everybody," he calls out.

"Hi, Ted," Ella says. "Is this official, or are you looking for a glass of lemonade?"

Ted's dark handlebar mustache makes it impossible to read his demeanor. "No time for lemonade, Miss Ella," he says. "But thanks anyway. This is official business. I got a registered letter here for Tucker."

CHAPTER TWO

With an air of authority, Ted walks up to Tucker's chair and turns his clipboard toward her. "You'll need to sign here," he says. Taking a pen from behind his ear, he hands it to her and points to the appropriate line.

Tucker folds her arms across her chest. "I ain't signin' nothin' 'til I know what it is. What's in there?"

Ted rolls his eyes. "Lord have mercy, Tucker. Does everything have to be a hassle with you? How should I know what's in the envelope? Just sign the form, will you? I've got other mail to deliver."

"What if'n I don't sign it? What then?"

Ted looks pleadingly at Ella and Carter. "How do ya'll deal with this woman?" Turning back to Tucker, he says, "If you don't sign it, then it will get reported back to the sender that you refused to do so."

Unfolding her arms, Tucker jerks the clipboard out of Ted's hand. "Give it here! I'll sign the damn thing."

She slowly etches her name on the postal form and then hands the clipboard back to Ted.

He gives Tucker the letter. "Thank you so much," he says sarcastically. As he turns to leave he says, "I hope the rest of ya'll have a nice day."

"See you 'round, Ted," says Carter.

They watch as Ted's car departs in a cloud of dust and then turn their attention on Tucker. She has folded the letter in half and is stuffing it into the back pocket of her pants.

"I'd like t' hear m' April sing another song," Tucker says. "Ya'll kick another'n off."

"Whatever you say," Ella replies. Reaching for her Autoharp, she asks, "What do you want to sing, April?"

"What about some Jimi Hendrix?" August says with a laugh.

"I don't know about him," Ella says. "Do you think anyone can sing right who plays backwards?"

"Huh?" August says.

Eyes twinkling, Ella says, "You know he plays left-handed, don't you? Well, that's backwards. Everyone knows that."

August's eyes widen. "You know who Jimi Hendrix is, Miss Ella?"

"Of course I do," she replies. "I'm interested in all kinds of music. It's just that this old-timey music we play takes me back to a simpler time in my life. It pulls at my heart to hear April's clear voice sending the words and notes on a journey down my memory lane." Placing the palm of her hand on her chest, she adds, "It touches me right here."

Shady Green breaks into the moment. "'Et's do ''Alty Dog.'"

Everyone else puzzles over Shady's meaning, but April quickly picks it up. "That's one of my favorites!" she says energetically. "Kick off 'Salty Dog' for us, Mr. Carter."

As Smiley Carter plays the introduction, April starts clogging across the wooden porch. She makes her way to Tucker, grabs Tucker's thick hands, and tries to swing her arms in rhythm as she begins singing—"Standing on the corner with the lowdown blues, a great big hole in the bottom of my shoes. Honey let me be your salty dog."

When Tucker doesn't respond, April rests her head on Tucker's chest. Looking coyly up into her face, April continues the song. "Look it here, Sal, I know you, a hole in your stocking and a wore out shoe. Honey let me be your salty dog."

August claps in time to the music.

Ella stretches out and taps one leg of Tucker's chair with her foot, never losing the rhythm on her Autoharp. When Tucker looks her way, Ella mouths, "You sing."

Forgetting herself, Tucker allows the music to sweep her up. She gets lost in its vortex. Looking down at April, Tucker opens her mouth and, in perfect rhythm, sings, "Down in the wildwood sitting on a log, finger on the trigger and an eye on the hog. Honey let me be your salty dog."

Whoops and hollers of surprise and delight erupt from everyone on the porch, and they all join in singing the chorus. "Let me be your salty dog or I won't be your man at all. Honey let me be your salty dog."

After two more verses they all pause to catch their breath.

April beams as she climbs up and perches on Tucker's leg.

Smiley Carter pulls a blue bandanna from his hip pocket and wipes the sweat off his face. "Tucker," he says, "I've known you most my whole life and I don't reckon I ever heard you sing. You got a nice high tenor voice. Yes, mighty fine. April, I guess you got your pretty voice from your grandmama Tucker."

Tucker looks at Ella and says, "Don't fergit. April's gotta another grandma who knows a thing 'r two 'bout music."

The two women exchange a slight nod of acknowledgment.

"Well, now," Carter says. "That's true, that's true. I still sometimes forget about that. April, I guess you got a double dose of musical genes from your grandmamas."

April slides off Tucker's leg and walks over to March. Touching him on the shoulder she says, "I noticed you didn't sing with us. Is something wrong?"

Jerking away from her touch, March stands up. His eyes are slits, and his eyebrows are knitted together. "Wrong?" he says. "Why does something always have to be wrong? No! Nothing's wrong!" Stomping off the porch, he heads toward the road.

Carter clears his throat loudly. "Shady, I believe it's 'bout time for me to head home. You coming with me?"

Surprised, Shady says, "'ut ah thought—"

"Whatever you thought," Carter cuts in, "it was wrong." He lifts his banjo from around his neck and places it gently in its red velvet-lined black case. Shady follows his lead and eases the body of his guitar into a pillow-case, tying it off halfway up the neck with a piece of grass string.

Carter waves and says, "You ladies have a good evenin'. We need to do this again real soon. It does my ol' heart good."

"Mine, too," Ella agrees. Smiling, she says, "And who knows what song we might hear out of Tucker next time."

A corner of Tucker's mouth twitches ever so slightly. Tilting her head up a bit, she says, "It must be these here new glasses. Things ain't been quite th' same since I got 'em."

Tucker and Ella watch Carter drive off on his tractor with Shady Green and August each perched on the rear tire fenders.

Slapping both hands on her thighs, Tucker rises from her chair. "Guess I better head home, too, an' see what kind o' bee March got in his bonnet."

Ella gets up with her. "Let me walk with you to the road. April, will you carry all the glasses inside?"

"Yes, ma'am," April replies.

As Tucker and Ella walk across the yard, Ella says, "It's none of my business, but I'm worried about March."

"How so?" Tucker asks.

"Well, August has found his father and is spending lots of time with Carter. April has found additional family, too. She practically lives with me. Maisy was all March had and now she's gone. It must be awfully confusing to him."

Tucker stops when they get to the road. Facing Ella, she says, "Don't guess I ever thought much 'bout that. He's always been a pain in th' ass. I just figured it was more o' th' same. March just bein' March. He needs t' git his head outta his butt an' quit feelin' sorry fer 'imself."

"I suppose," Ella says slowly. "Anyway, like I said, it's none of my business. I'm sure you'll handle it."

Tucker folds her arms across her chest. "I heared that tone o' voice outta you b'fore. If'n y' got somethin' on yore mind, spit it out."

Ella looks warily at Tucker. "Well," she begins, "I hear there are some people who have been taking their children to a child psychologist in Jackson and he's really helping them."

"Hmph!" Tucker grunts and spits a stream of tobacco juice. "The day I need somebody t' tell me how t' handle m' kids is th' day I'll quit chewin' tobacco. I best be goin'." She strides toward her house.

Speaking to Tucker's retreating back, Ella says, "It was just an idea. You don't have to get all in a huff about it."

CHAPTER THREE

The sun has relinquished its hold on the day by the time Tucker arrives at her house. She moves carefully as she climbs the steps to the porch in the dim twilight. She notices that the inside of the house is dark.

Just as she grips the front doorknob she hears the chain on the porch swing give a quiet jingle. Turning, she sees a figure sitting in the seat.

"That you, March?" she asks.

"Yes'm," March replies quietly.

"Care if'n I join y'?" Tucker asks.

"It's your swing," he says curtly.

"Watch yore mouth!" Tucker snaps. "I's jes' askin'."

She ambles toward him as the evening's darkness gains further control. March scoots over to give her room to sit beside him. She sits with a grunt. The chains of the swing dance in response to the abrupt change in weight.

Tucker and March slowly swing in silence as night fills the air with its own kind of music. The chuck-will's-widow begins its frenetic call. In the distance a screech owl imitates a woman's scream.

Crickets and tree frogs provide the accompaniment. Occasionally a bullfrog punctuates the serenade with its deep bass voice.

"Seems like," Tucker begins abruptly, "y' got somethin' stuck in yore craw. It's best y' jes' spit it out. Elsewise it's gonna fester an' eat a hole in y'."

March blurts out, "Everybody got a new family but me! It's not fair! And April and August act like they don't even miss Mama." His voice begins to break. "Nobody ever talks about her."

Tucker hears him sniff. "Fair," she says softly. Reaching her arm around his shoulders, she pulls him to her side. "I 'member a time in m' life when I was mad about things not bein' fair. It was like that fer a long time fer me. That was until I figured out life ain't never gonna be fair. There ain't nothin' fair 'bout life, March. Y' need t' understand that an' accept it."

"What do you mean, 'ain't nothin' fair 'bout life'?" March asks. "How can you say that?"

Tucker is silent. Images of her childhood flash through her memory and strike her heart like hailstones in a summer storm.

She considers March. She wonders if she should share her story with him. Is it any of his business? What would Ella say to do?

Tucker carefully ventures a step into her story, like someone testing the thickness of ice on a pond. "I decided when I was sixteen years ol' that life wasn't never gonna be fair. An' I ain't never been surprised 'r disappointed since."

The sounds of the night envelop them again as March tries to digest Tucker's pithy statements.

"Tucker," he says tentatively, "what happened to you when you was growing up? What happened when you were sixteen that made you know life would never be fair?"

Tucker stiffens and she stops the swing. She feels as if she's about to fall off the roof of a tall barn. Her chest tightens.

March feels the tension and holds his breath, expecting any moment for Tucker to knock him out of the swing or yell at him.

Unexpectedly, Tucker starts the swing going again. "It ain't fittin' fer th' ears o' children," she finally says.

March pulls away and shifts so he is facing her. "I am not a child! I'm almost a teenager. Don't I have a right to know?"

Tucker pushes the swing a little harder. "Hmmm," she says. "Never thought 'bout it like that. A 'right to know'? Maybe y' do. Maybe y' do."

March eases into the crook of Tucker's arm.

"March," Tucker begins, "the man I knew as m' daddy was th' sorriest piece o' trash that ever walked this earth. He worked me like an animal on this here farm. It wasn't nothin' fer me t' come home from school when I was nine years old and chop cotton by moonlight. Many times I was still in th' field when th' sun come up th' next mornin' and I'd have to go to school without havin' no sleep.

"I learnt early not t' tell him no. He'd strip m' clothes off and beat me with whatever he grabbed holt of—stick, tree branch, balin' wire, leather reins—didn't matter t' him. I tol'ja one time about him puttin' me in th' dog pen fer two weeks. I eat and drunk what th' dogs had.

"But that ain't th' worst of it—" Tucker pauses for the first time in her story. Her heart is hammering against her chest like the mallets of a kettledrum. She feels flushed. Using her free hand, she reaches and tugs at the collar of her shirt, hoping it will help her find her breath, which has suddenly become labored.

March is holding his breath, too. The air is electric. Finding her voice, Tucker continues, "This is hard t' say, March, 'cause I don't know how much you know about things—about boys and girls. It's what he done 'tween m' legs . . . that's th' worst thing."

"No!" March cries out. He claps his hand over Tucker's mouth. "Don't say it, Tucker! Don't say it!"

Tucker twists her head to get free of March's desperate effort to muffle her.

"You's th' one what wanted t' hear this," she says angrily.

March turns his back to her. "I've heard enough. I don't want to hear any more." His sobs punctuate his words. "I'm sorry for what was done to you. I'm sorry I've been so much trouble for you. I'm just so sorry for everything."

He jumps out of the swing and rushes through the front door of the house. The screen door adds its own exclamation point to the scene as it slaps shut behind him.

Stunned by March's reaction and shocked at how much of her secret life she let out from where she'd hidden it for so long, Tucker sits motionless in the swing. Even the tree frogs and crickets seem to have been shocked into silence.

The cool, damp night air finds its way inside Tucker's shirt, causing her to shudder. She rises stiffly from the swing and walks slowly to the front door. Going inside, she catches the screen door before it slaps shut behind her.

Listening closely, she hears March in his room upstairs preparing for bed. She walks up the first two steps of the staircase and stops. After a moment, a sigh escapes her and she backs down the steps and retreats to her bedroom.

The next morning, Tucker flips the eggs in her iron skillet and hollers, "Last call, March! These eggs is gonna be done in a minute. Now git yore butt down here!"

Carrying the skillet to the table she slides two fried eggs onto each plate, their dark yellow yolks looking like twin suns. The skillet lands with a heavy clang as she pitches it back on the stove.

She casts an eye toward the kitchen doorway, then jerks her chair from under the table and sits down. Grabbing her fork, she starts cutting up her egg, the yolk now set free to run across her plate in dark, yellow rivulets.

"That boy," she mutters under her breath. "I'm 'bout tired o' his laziness in th' mornin'."

She takes a bite of egg and washes it down with strong black coffee. "March!" she yells.

The silence of the house swallows her challenge.

Slamming her fork on the table, she yells, "That's it. I'm fixin' t' come drag you outta yore bed and down them stairs."

She rises, knocking her chair over.

Her heavy boots sound like a bass drum as she pounds up the stairs. She bursts through the door to March's bedroom. "I said—"

She stops. March is nowhere to be seen. She notices his smoothly made bed. The open door of his closet reveals that it is empty.

"March?" she says softly.

In a daze she moves to his chest of drawers. It takes a couple of tugs to get the top drawer to open. It is empty except for a folded piece of paper.

"Oh my Lord, no," Tucker says in a whisper. Her hand trembles as she reaches for the paper. She closes her eyes but tears squeeze from them anyway.

She finally opens her eyes and unfolds the paper. On it she reads:

I'm the most horrible person on the face of God's earth. I've done terrible things. Nobody wants me. I don't deserve to be here. Please forgive me. —March

CHAPTER FOUR

April steps softly toward the end of the couch Ella is sitting on. She notices the open book in Ella's lap and her thin hand holding it open. Ella's head is bowed low and she hasn't turned a page in a while.

"Grandmother?" April says gently.

Ella doesn't respond.

Touching Ella's hand, April says a little louder, "Grandmother?"

Ella's head comes up slowly. Her eyes are red and unfocused. "Huh?" she says.

April crawls onto the couch and sits on her knees beside Ella. She takes Ella's hands in hers. "It's me, Grandmother. It's April."

Ella turns to look at April. She smiles, her eyes clearing now. "But of course it is. I guess I dozed off, didn't I? You wouldn't think washing breakfast dishes would tire a person out. But I didn't sleep very well last night, so I guess it caught up with me."

Frowning, April says, "You seem like you're tired a lot of the time. Are you okay?"

Ella closes her book and pulls April tightly to her. "Yes, yes, I'm all right. Don't you worry about me. Now, what's on your mind?"

April drops her head and says in a whisper, "It's nothing."

Ella puts two fingers under April's chin and gently lifts until they are looking into each other's eyes. "Anything you have to say to me or ask me is always something. It's never *nothing*. You are important to me."

April swallows and says, "Where is my mother?"

Furrows appear on Ella's forehead. "April, you know Maisy died two years ago. Don't you remember?"

Unfolding her legs, April shifts to a more natural sitting position beside Ella. She picks up one of Ella's hands and softly traces the veins on the back of it with her finger. After a moment she says, "Oh, I know she died. But where is she now? Is she under the ground in the cemetery? I wonder what she looks like now. Sometimes I have scary dreams about that."

"No, no, no," Ella says quickly. "She's not still in the ground. Well, sort of . . . but not like you think." She pauses, then, half aloud says, "This is hard to explain."

"How come?" April asks.

"How come what?"

"How come it's hard to explain?"

"Because it's something that even adults have a difficult time understanding. And when we don't understand something clearly, it makes it very hard to put it into words that make sense. But let me try.

"You know how we enjoy the vegetables from Tucker's garden?"

April nods her head.

"Well," Ella continues, "where do those vegetables come from? I mean, how do those plants get there?"

April frowns and cocks her head to one side. She looks toward the ceiling. Suddenly she smiles and says, "From the seeds we all plant in the spring."

"Exactly," Ella agrees. "You may not know this, but putting that seed in the ground actually causes it to die. But just before it dies, it releases something that's been hiding in it its whole life. It's something no one can see. It's the beautiful plant that finds its way upward into the brilliant sunshine above the ground. That beautiful plant comes from that plain-looking seed."

April stares, thinking about Ella's description.

"Now when a person dies," Ella says, "they release something that's been inside of them their entire life, too. It's been there, unseen, since they were in their mother's womb. We call it the spirit. When the person dies, that spirit is set free."

"Why didn't I see Mama's spirit?" April asks.

"This is one reason it is hard to explain," Ella replies. "We are not able to see a person's spirit. I guess you'd have to say it is invisible to us."

"Like a ghost?" April asks, eyes wide.

"Maybe, sort of. But not like the kind that you read about in books and see in movies. Not ghosts that haunt places and scare people. I don't think there's such thing as ghosts."

April looks intently at Ella, scanning her face to see if she is joking.

"So," April says, "what happens to the spirit? Where does it go?"

"That's my April," Ella says with a smile. "Always full of questions. The spirit goes back to where it came from in the first place. It goes to God, and he decides where it should go to live."

"How do you know all this, Grandmother?" April asks.

"When I was a little girl like you, I went to church all the time. I read the Bible and listened to my preacher. I loved it." Ella's eyes begin to redden. In a distant voice she says, "But that was a long time ago."

The sound of heavy boots on the porch breaks in on their moment.

"Who in the—" Ella begins. But her voice is halted by someone pounding so hard on her door that it rattles the windows.

"Ella! Ella McDade!" The shrill, panicked voice of Tucker comes from the other side.

"Quickly, April," Ella says, "open the door."

Darting to the door, April grabs the knob and flings the door open.

Ella immediately notices Tucker's crimson face and her heaving chest. Her friend is leaning against the door frame, supporting herself with one hand. Then Ella spies a crumpled piece of paper in Tucker's other hand.

Tucker opens her mouth to speak but is unable to catch her breath.

"Tucker," Ella says, "come in and sit down. April, go get a glass of water. Quickly."

Ella moves to Tucker's side and says, "Lean on me and let me help you to the chair."

When Tucker puts her weight on Ella, Ella bends, unprepared for Tucker's weight. But, like a willow tree flexing its slender boughs, she rises back up and, grunting, assists Tucker to a chair.

April arrives and offers the glass of water to Tucker. Tucker grabs it with both hands and gulps it down between gasps.

When Tucker has finished the water, she looks to the ceiling and wails, "Lord, Lord, what else is going to happen to me?"

Ella kneels in front of Tucker and places her hands on Tucker's knees. "Tucker, look at me."

But Tucker's eyes are unfocused.

Digging her fingernails into Tucker's thighs, Ella repeats, "Look at me!"

The sharp pain draws Tucker's attention to Ella. She blinks rapidly. Glancing at April and then back to Ella, she says in a hoarse whisper, "It's . . . it's . . . March . . ."

April moves to Tucker's side, grips her thick bicep with both hands, and shakes her. With panic in her voice, she asks, "What about March?"

Tucker thrusts her hand toward Ella. Unclenching her fist, she reveals the crumpled note from March. "He's gone."

Snatching the note, Ella says, "What? What do you mean he's gone? You're making no sense." She quickly reads the note. Slowly she looks up into Tucker's eyes. The note floats to the floor like a falling leaf.

April grabs it before it lands and reads it.

"Talk to me, Tucker," Ella says gently.

"I kept callin' 'im fer breakfast this mornin'. Then I went up t' 'is room thinkin' he was just bein' lazy and wouldn't git up. As soon as I walked in I could tell somethin' wadn't right. His bed wadn't never slept in. All 'is clothes was gone. I opened 'is dresser an' found th' note."

Tears stream down her cheeks and drop onto her brown Dickies shirt. The darkened spots they leave are like the dark stains on her heart. "What am I goin' t' do, Ella? What am I goin' t' do?"

Ella stands up and begins pacing. "First things first. Is it possible he went to someone's house? Could he have gone to see August?"

"August?" Tucker says faintly.

"Yes," Ella says emphatically. "Maybe he just went to Smiley Carter's house to see August." She moves to her phone. "I'm going to call over there to see if they've seen him."

CHAPTER FIVE

Placing the phone receiver back in its cradle, Ella slowly turns to face the expectant Tucker and April. "He's not there. They haven't seen him since yesterday afternoon when everyone was here. But they are coming right over so we can figure out what to do."

April drops her head and rubs her eyes as she cries. Her long, golden hair hides her reddening face.

Tucker notices her and says, "Come here, child." She opens her arms to receive April.

April shakes her head and runs to her bedroom, slamming the door behind her.

Ella and Tucker look at each other.

"She's just upset," Ella says. "Maybe she just needs to be alone for a bit and cry."

"I spec' you're right," Tucker agrees.

Clapping her hands together, Ella exclaims, "Ron Harris! I need to call Sheriff Harris!"

She grabs the phone and dials the number from memory. After a pause she says, "This is Ella McDade. I need to speak to the sheriff. It's an emergency."

There is a pause, and then she says, "Ron, this is Ella McDade. We've got a situation out here. It appears March Tucker has run away from home."

She listens and then replies, "Yes, that's Tucker's youngest grandson. She found the bedroom empty this morning and a note that indicates he's run away. He must have left during the night."

As she listens to the sheriff, a seldom-seen scowl comes over Ella's face, and she places her free hand on her hip. "I don't want a deputy," she says flatly. "I want you to come out. Please."

His reply evidently pleases her and her scowl disappears. Her voice shifts, "Oh, thank you, Ron. It really means a lot to me. We're all at my house. I'll see you in a bit."

Hanging up the phone, Ella smiles at Tucker and says, "Ron will know what to do. He'll help us find March. How about some coffee? Would you like some?"

Tucker pushes herself out of the chair and ambles toward the kitchen. "That'd be good."

Ella pours water into her CorningWare percolator. After spooning coffee into its metal basket, she places the pot on the stove.

Tucker glances out the window. "I b'lieve I see Smiley Carter comin' over th' hill on 'is tractor." Squinting, she adds, "Looks like August is comin' with' im."

"Why doesn't Carter own a pickup truck or a car?" Ella asks. "He drives that tractor everywhere he goes."

"He's jes' curious that way," Tucker replies. "He tol' me once it didn't make no sense t' own two means o' transportation. An' since y' can't plow a garden with a truck, he'd rather have a tractor."

Smiling, Ella shakes her head and says, "I guess there's no arguing with that kind of logic."

At the sound of the tractor pulling into Ella's front yard, both women walk to the front door. Ella opens the door and they step onto the front porch just as Carter is turning off the tractor.

August springs off the tractor and runs to Tucker and Ella. Frantically he looks from face to face. "Is it true? Has March really run away?"

Folding her arms across her chest, Tucker says, "Appears he has. Y' know anythin' 'bout that?"

August's expression changes from one of concern to one of confusion. "Huh? What do you mean?"

Carter walks up behind him. "Hey, ladies. What do you think happened to the boy?"

Ella looks at Tucker.

Tucker's gaze remains fixed on August. "Y' heard me. Do y' know anythin' 'bout this? Is this somethin' y' an' March planned?"

Carter moves beside August. "Easy now, Tucker," he says. "Ain't no sense in accusin' folks with no reason."

Tucker's head snaps toward Carter. "You listen here. Y' may be this boy's daddy, but I raised 'im. And I'll ask 'im anythin' I damn well want to."

Ella notices Carter's reaction. His eyes close to a tight squint and one of his hands closes into a fist. As he starts to take a step toward Tucker, Ella steps in front of Tucker and says, "Let's all go inside and put our heads together to see if we can figure where March may have gone to. Sheriff Harris will be here shortly, too, and he'll have all sorts of questions for all of us, I'm sure."

Taking Tucker by the arm, Ella forcibly turns her around and nudges her toward the door. Behind her she hears Carter speaking in low, muffled tones to August. "I don't know, boy. She's just upset, I guess. Don't pay her no mind."

As they all go inside, the smell of fresh coffee greets them.

"Let's go sit at the kitchen table while I pour us some coffee," Ella says.

"That does sound like a good idea," Carter says. Looking around, he asks, "Where's little April?"

"She's closed off in 'er room," Tucker replies. "She's awful upset. Me an' Ella decided it might be best t' leave 'er alone fer a bit an' let 'er cry some."

Carter looks at August. Placing his hand on the boy's shoulder, he says, "Maybe you ought to go talk to your sister an' comfort 'er. You're the oldest. It might help."

August jerks away from Carter's touch. "I don't think so," he says. "She don't want to see me. I wouldn't know what to say anyway."

A puzzled expression passes across Ella's face as she looks at August. *Is it worry over his brother's disappearance that has him so on edge? Or is there something going on that he's not telling?*

Carter and Tucker exchange a look. Tucker shrugs her shoulders.

"Okay, okay," Carter says soothingly to August, "you don't have to go see her."

Ella places coffee cups on the table and pours them each a cup.

Everyone settles into their chairs and takes a sip, except for Carter.

"Miss Ella . . ." he begins.

"Oh, Carter!" Ella exclaims, "I forgot your saucer." She gets up, retrieves a saucer from the cabinet, and hands it to him.

Smiling warmly, Carter says, "Thank you."

Patting his hand, Ella says, "You're welcome."

Tucker notices that Ella's hand seems to linger on Carter's hand longer than necessary.

Carter sets the saucer on the table and then dribbles coffee into it from the cup until the coffee is almost to the rim. Picking up the saucer with both hands, he slowly brings it to his mouth and gently blows it. Then he sips the coffee from the saucer, making loud slurping sounds as he does.

Tucker looks from Carter to Ella. Her eyes blink rapidly. She opens her mouth to speak, but suddenly the sound of closing car doors focuses everyone's attention.

Ella says, "It must be Ron Harris." She gets up and reaches the door just as someone knocks.

As Ella opens the door, the broad frame of Sheriff Ron Harris fills the doorway. He steps inside without waiting for an invitation.

"Hi, Ron," Ella says. She glances up at the Stetson hat perched on his head.

"Sorry," he says as he removes his hat. "Who all is here?"

"We're in the kitchen," Ella replies. "Come on in and I'll pour you some coffee."

As the sheriff enters the kitchen he nods briefly at Smiley Carter and August, but locks eyes with Tucker. "Before anyone tells me anything," he says, "I want to hear the story from you."

CHAPTER SIX

After I found th' note in 'is drawer," Tucker concludes her story to the sheriff, "I come down here t' Ella's as fast as I could."

"So," the sheriff begins, "the last time you saw him was last night when he went upstairs to bed, right?"

"That's right," Tucker says.

"What about the rest of you?" the sheriff asks, looking round the table. "When's the last time any of you saw him?"

"Last time I seen him," Carter replies, "was here at Miss Ella's yesterday evening. We had us a jam session on the porch and March was here with Tucker."

Nodding, Ella says, "Yes, that's the last time I saw him, too."

Sheriff Harris turns his gaze to August.

"That's the last time I seen him, too," August says. "How come everybody keeps looking at me? I don't know anything about what happened to him."

A movement catches the sheriff's eye. Turning, he sees April slowly walking into the room.

She stands between Ella and Tucker. Each of her grandmothers takes one of her hands. Her face is blotchy and her nose is red from crying.

"April," Harris says gently. "Do you know anything about where March might be?"

"She don't know nothin'," Tucker interjects in a harsh tone. "She's upset. Leave 'er alone."

Without taking his eyes off of April, Harris says to Tucker, "Let's let April answer for herself."

Dropping her head, April says quietly, "I don't know where he is. I'm scared."

The sheriff scans the group. "So, was there anyone else pickin' and grinnin' with you all last evening?"

"Shady Green was here," Ella says.

"He come with me," Smiley Carter adds. "And I took him home, too."

Getting up from the table, Harris says, "Let's all go out on the porch." Walking toward the door, he continues, "I want everyone to think back to yesterday evening. Try to remember everything that happened."

Everyone follows the sheriff outside. A young deputy leans against the sheriff's patrol car. He has close-cropped hair and is wearing dark sunglasses. He straightens up quickly upon seeing the sheriff.

"This is my newest deputy, Kenny King. You all remember his dad, Luke King. He owned the Big K Grocery. He's been discharged from the army, was an MP for them. We're lucky to have him."

The young deputy smiles and nods politely to the group.

"Hey, Kenny," Carter says. "I knew your granddaddy, Harless King. Welcome back from 'Nam."

"Thank you, sir," Kenny replies.

Harris faces the group. "Was there anything that was done or said yesterday that might have upset March? Think hard."

Tucker and Ella look at each other. It's all Ella can do to control her urge to blurt out to the sheriff her impressions of March from yesterday and to tell him about her conversation with Tucker.

Tucker speaks up. "He was in a foul mood b'fore we got down here. And it didn't get no better once we got here."

"She's speakin' the truth," Carter says. "The boy looked like he had a storm cloud hanging over his head when they walked up to the porch. Almost like he wanted to fight somebody."

Harris turns his attention to Tucker. "So what happened that put him in such a disagreeable mood?"

Tucker shakes her head and says, "Lord if I know. All I did was rub some dirt off him when we was walkin' down here. Seems like he's been in a bad mood since 'is mama was killed."

"Hmmm," Harris muses. He unfolds March's note and studies it again. "'I've done terrible things,' March says here." Looking at Tucker, he quizzes her, "What does he mean by that?"

April grips Ella's hand so tightly that Ella winces in pain. It is the grip of someone with a conscience wrapped in regret.

Nervously, August steps closer to Carter.

Tucker folds her arms across her chest. "I ain't no mind reader. I don't know what he meant by that. He's one who's always in trouble, either at home 'r school. What I don't git is why you're standin' 'round here talkin' instead o' gettin' out there lookin' fer th' boy."

The sheriff slowly puts his Stetson on. Hands on his hips, he says, "And exactly which direction do you suggest we start our search? There's three hundred and sixty degrees on a compass. That's three hundred and sixty directions we could set off in."

"Th' way I figure it," Tucker retorts, "y' git paid good money t' know what t' do in these situations."

"Look, Tucker, I'm just here to help. Let's go up to your house to see if Kenny and I can find some clues. Bubba Garrett is supposed to be meeting us there in a bit with his bloodhounds. We're going to see if they can strike a trail."

Walking to his cruiser, he says, "Kenny, let Tucker sit in the front with me. You slide into the back."

"Yes, sir," Kenny replies as he opens the car door for Tucker. After she gets inside, he shuts the door and then takes his place in the backseat.

Ella, April, Smiley Carter, and August watch from the porch as the sheriff's car drives off toward Tucker's house. They stand silently for several moments.

Carter clears his throat and says, "What should we do, Miss Ella? Do you think we need to go to Tucker's and help search?"

"I hardly know myself," Ella replies. "I believe Ron would've asked us to go up there if he thought we could help. I don't know if he just got so frustrated with Tucker that he didn't think to ask us or what."

As she is speaking, a pickup truck speeds by with a cloud of dust. The deep barking of Bubba Garrett's bloodhounds can be heard through the dust.

"Those are some good dogs," Carter says. "There's some amazing stories 'bout how they can even track through water. If March is on the ground somewhere, them dogs'll be the ones that finds him."

"You really think so?" August asks.

Putting his arm around the boy's shoulders, Carter says, "Oh sure. March just got a wild hair about something. He's probably on his way back home as we speak. Don't you worry."

"Can you and I go on up there?" August asks. "I know the fields and woods around there like the back of my hand."

"Well, sure," Carter replies. "It sure can't hurt." Turning to Ella and April, he says, "Why don't you all stay here by the phone in case somebody needs something?"

"That's a good idea," Ella says. "You all run along."

April stands in front of Ella as Carter and August ride off on the tractor. Ella gently places her hands on April's shoulders.

April flinches at Ella's touch. Shaking her head, she says quietly, "It's my fault."

Ella turns April around to face her. "What did you say?"

"It's my fault that March ran away," April says. She tries to walk past Ella.

Ella moves to block her path and squats down to be eye level with her. Taking April's hands in hers, she says, "Wait. What do you mean by that?"

"It doesn't matter," April says, defeated. "What's done is done." She jerks away from Ella and runs inside the house, slamming the front door behind her.

After a moment, Ella hears from deep within the house the muted sound of April's bedroom door slamming shut, too.

CHAPTER SEVEN

Shielding her eyes from the sun with her hand, Tucker stands on her front porch looking at the retreating backs of the sheriff, his deputy, and Bubba Garrett. Every few steps Bubba almost stumbles because his dogs pull so hard against their leashes. Their deep baying sounds like a duet from a mournful, operatic scene.

Lowering her hand, Tucker turns toward the sound of Carter's approaching tractor. He rolls up to her porch with August perched on a rear fender.

"Where are they?" Augusts asks as he leaps to the ground before the tractor comes to a stop.

When Carter shuts off his engine the sound of distant barking can be heard. "Is that them?" August asks.

"It is," Tucker answers. "As soon as I let th' dogs smell one o' March's shirts they lit right into 'is scent and commenced t' bayin'."

"Looks like they're headed sorta in the direction of town, don't it?" Carter asks.

Tucker nods her head. "Could be. But that's also th' direction o' th' Paris Highway. So it's hard t' tell where th' boy was headed."

Suddenly August starts running in the direction the search party has gone.

"August!" Tucker's train-whistle voice cuts through the air. "Where you goin'?"

August calls back over his shoulder, "They've got to go through Macauley's woods. I'm going to go help them." He lowers his head and runs with the speed of a gazelle, leaping over puddles and furrows.

"August!" Tucker yells.

"Leave him be, Tucker," Carter says. "It's his brother. He's got to do something to help. Sittin' by and doin' nothin' would be the worst thing for him."

Folding her arms across her chest, Tucker stares back into the sun. Then she turns and ambles to her porch swing, where she drops heavily into the seat.

Carter lowers his large frame to the sun-bleached floor of the porch and leans against one of the cedar posts. Taking out his Case pocketknife, he unfolds the smallest blade and begins digging at a stubborn splinter in the palm of his hand.

Tucker watches him for several moments before saying, "Y' better let me git y' some tweezers or you're gonna dig a hole plumb through yore hand. How long has it been stuck in there?"

Carter answers without looking up. "I don't know for sure, maybe a week. I think it's a locust thorn that broke off deep inside. I was cutting some fence posts and must have done it then. I think it's gotten infected."

Grunting, Tucker gets out of the swing. "Locust, huh? That sure 'nough means it's infected or gonna be. Them makes some mighty sore places if'n y' don't treat it. I'll git some tweezers and some coal oil."

Carter shakes his hand gingerly. "You're right about it being sore. I don't know what makes a worse sore, a locust thorn or getting finned by a catfish. But they's both bad news."

In a moment Tucker returns from inside the house. She approaches Carter and says, "Well, stand up here if'n y' want me t' fix it. I sure ain't gonna git down on th' floor 'cause I'd never git back up."

Carter snaps shut his pocketknife and uses the porch post to help him get to a standing position. He offers his hand to Tucker.

Tucker grabs it roughly and tilts the palm toward the sunlight. A small smile dances at the corners of her mouth. Seizing the tweezers tightly, she says, "Ain't'chu glad I got these new glasses? Otherwise, ain't no tellin' what I might grab holt of."

"Just do what you got to do and quit talking," Carter says. "And be easy. That thing is—"

Before he finishes, Tucker drives the tweezers deep into his palm.

"Ow!" Carter cries.

"Oh, hush!" Tucker says. "You sound like a baby." With a flourish she jerks the splinter out of Carter's palm.

They both look closely as she rolls it off the tweezers onto her own palm.

"Looks like you's right," Tucker says, "it's a locust thorn all right." Pulling a pint jar from between her side and arm, she says, "Gimme yore hand again."

Carter offers his hand as if it is a sacrificial lamb.

Grabbing his wrist, Tucker says, "Oh my Lord, fer a grown man you're mighty skittish. Now hold it over th' side o' th' porch. I don't want this coal oil t' git all over th' floor."

Carter winces as the coal oil splashes onto his hand.

Tucker takes her thumb and vigorously rubs his wound. "Now ya'll be good t' go in a day 'r two. Takes that long fer th' soreness t' leave."

Carter reaches into his back pocket, takes out a red bandanna, and wraps it around his hand. "Let me say right here and now,"

Carter begins. "Don't never try to hire yourself out as a nurse. Your curing is about as bad as the hurting is."

Tucker returns to her swing. "I'll tell y' what y' can do next time," she says. "Y' can let yore hand rot off fer all I care. Not even a thankye?"

"You're right," Carter says apologetically. "Thank you. I'm sure I'll be pleased in a few days that you helped me. It's just hard to see that when I'm hurting so." He walks to the end of the porch and looks into the distance. "I can't hear them dogs no more. They've either lost the trail or they've run out of earshot."

When Tucker doesn't reply, he returns to his place on the porch and lowers himself to the floor.

The next hour passes in silence.

Tucker replays in her mind her conversation on the porch last night with March. *Did I say too much? How come he got s' upset when I tried t' tell 'im what m' daddy done t' me? Could it be somebody has done abused him?* At that question her face flushes and she clenches both fists.

Carter breaks into the silence. "Wonder what got into ol' March that made him run off like this?"

Tucker tries to orient herself back into the moment. She takes a deep breath and says, "Who can plumb th' depths o' a child's mind? I sometimes think th' older I git th' less I know 'bout anythin'. Tryin' t' make sense outta life wears me out. I'm weary o' it."

Carter cocks his head as he mulls over Tucker's words. Shaking his head slowly, he says, "You for sure ain't never had nothing come easy in your life. I can say that for certain. But you know what? I ain't never heard you complain about it. I mean, you might be mad about something happening, but you're not one of those complaining, bitter old women. That's pretty remarkable."

Tucker looks at her old friend and one corner of her mouth lifts up slightly. "Who you callin' ol'?"

A brief, deep laugh springs out of Carter. "Well, you is. And me, too." Taking off his cap and rubbing his white hair, he adds, "That's what all this snow on the mountaintops says." He points a finger at Tucker's white hair for emphasis.

"Let me tell y' 'bout this white hair," Tucker says as she pulls on a lock of her hair. "Ever' one o' these hairs is a medal. They's medals for things I've had t' deal with an' overcome in m' life. I wear 'em proud. Besides, Miss Ella says m' white hair gives me character, whatever that means."

Genuine laughter flows from Carter. "Oh, you are a character all right. That's the truth if it's ever been told."

Tucker laughs with him.

When silence settles back on the couple, Carter says, "On the serious side, you've got a story to tell, Tucker."

"Wha'j' mean?"

"Your life story, that's what I'm talking about. It's a story about never giving up, about overcoming rough spots. It's the kind of story people need to hear."

"Hmph," Tucker grunts. "Wouldn't nobody b'lieve m' story. They'd think it was made up." As she finishes speaking, Tucker sits up sharply and squints in the twilight. "Do I see 'em comin' across th' field?"

Carter gets quickly to his feet and follows her gaze. After a long stare he says, "Sure 'nough. I believe it's them. They's got their flashlights on."

"How many is there?" Tucker asks as she gets out of the swing and walks to the end of the porch.

Carter joins her there. "There's one . . . two . . . three . . . and there's four; that's August. I can tell by his big Afro." Sadly, he adds, "But that's all I can see right now."

CHAPTER EIGHT

By the time the search party sets foot on the edge of Tucker's property there is only a dim glow in the western sky. The evening star has already shown its face. As Tucker and Carter wait anxiously on the porch, the approach of headlights arrests their attention.

The vehicle turns into Tucker's front yard, its lights sweeping across the scene like the spotlight from the high tower of a prison. The sharp edges of incongruent images flash in the harsh glare: White froth drips from the jowls of the exhausted bloodhounds. The pale faces of the sheriff and his deputy are streaked with dirt and sweat. Bubba's cheeks glow crimson. August's tall, thin form stands out from the beefy adults. The porcelain interior of a bathtub on its side glows back at the car. Old car tires throw shadows at odd angles. Tucker and Carter stand together, faces etched with concern.

When the driver extinguishes the headlights, the evening seems even darker. The door opens and the interior light reveals the familiar faces of Ella and April.

The search party, Ella, and April all arrive at the porch at the same time.

Questions punctuate the night air with the urgency that only fear can generate. Everyone speaks at once.

Tucker: "Wha'j' find?"

Carter: "August, are you okay?"

Ella: "Is March safe?"

Tucker: "Where ya'll been lookin'?"

Ella: "Did you see any signs of the boy?"

Carter: "How come ya'll come back?"

Sheriff Ron Harris's disembodied voice is heard from the darkness behind his flashlight. "Tucker, can we go inside where there's some light? And can we get some water for Bubba's dogs?"

"What's wrong with talkin' out here?" Tucker replies. "I can hear just as good outside as I can inside. I wanta know what happened."

Sensing her friend's reluctance to have people inside her house, Ella speaks up. "Tucker's right. There's more room out here and besides, you men will just track your dirt and mud inside. Tucker, let's you and me go inside and get everyone some water."

Ella takes a few halting steps. "Will someone please shine their flashlight so I can find my way to the porch? I've never seen such inconsideration."

Deputy King quickly switches on his flashlight. "I'm sorry, ma'am. Let me help."

By the time Ella reaches the porch, Tucker is opening the front door and switching on the inside light. "Thank you, Deputy," Ella says.

As Ella and Tucker disappear inside, Carter says, "August why don't you go draw a bucket of water for these here thirsty dogs?"

Before August can reply, April speaks up. "I'll go help you, August."

August is thankful that the darkness hides his startled reaction. "Uh, sure . . . okay. You come help me."

"You all need a flashlight?" the deputy asks.

"No, sir," August replies. "I done this so many times I could do it blindfolded."

As soon as the children step into the inky blackness and out of sight and hearing of the men, April whispers loudly to August, "Where is he?"

"Shhh!" August whispers back. "Keep your voice down. Everybody thinks I know something. Well, I don't."

As they get to the well behind the house, April says, "You and March have always had secret places you go to. Like the place you hide to smoke those grapevines."

"How do you know about that?"

"I followed you one time and saw you smoking."

August pours the water from the well into the bucket. "You better not tell," he says.

"I know how to keep secrets," April replies. "Me, you, and March have secrets. It's because of them that March has run away."

August freezes. "What are you talking about?"

"You know."

"Shut up!" August snaps. "Shut up, shut up, shut up! You don't know what you are talking about. Now come on and let's get this water to Bubba's dogs."

Meanwhile, at the front of the house, Carter says to the fatigued search party, "You boys come sit on the porch and take a load off. Ya'll look plumb tuckered out."

The faint light from inside Tucker's house spills through the windows in rectangular patches on the slatted floor of the porch. The shadows cast from the frames of the windowpanes paint skewed crucifixes on the men sitting below them.

In a moment, the screen door opens as Tucker pushes her way through, backside first. She holds the door back as Ella follows her. Tucker hands glass jars brimming with water to the sheriff, his deputy, and Bubba.

Ella takes a jar to Carter and sips one of her own.

Tucker turns in a circle. "Where's August and April?"

The two children emerge from the dark, August leaning to one side to offset the weight of the water bucket he is carrying. He sits it on the ground in front of the two dogs.

"Much obliged," Bubba says.

August and April join the group on the porch and Tucker offers them a jar of water to share.

"Okay," Tucker says, "is ever'body situated now? Will y' please tell me what happened an' why y' come back without March?"

"Well," the sheriff begins, "you saw how Bubba's dogs struck a trail right off. It appears March headed straight for Macauley's woods. I thought we might find him holed up there somewhere. You know how boys make hiding places and forts and things like that.

"He crossed back and forth over Mud Creek three or four times like he was deliberately trying to hide his scent from dogs that might follow him."

"That's so," Bubba says. "My dogs is probably the only ones in this area that could have kept up with him. I think the boy's been planning on running away for a while."

"That's just your opinion," Deputy King says in a low voice.

"Nobody knows anything for certain," Harris cuts in. "Anyway, we trailed him out of the woods and found where he'd been to Widow Harris's house."

"Are you for certain?" Ella asks.

"No doubt. He actually went inside and got some food out of her refrigerator." Shaking his head the sheriff adds, "I keep telling you people you need to start locking your houses at night."

"What'd he take?" Tucker asks.

"Huh?"

"What'd he take out o' 'er 'frig'?"

"Mrs. Harris said she was missing half of an apple pie and an entire block of cheese."

"That'd be 'im all right," Tucker muses. "Th' boy has a fondness fer both o' 'em."

"He followed the Paris Highway into town," the sheriff continues, "and then walked along old Highway 22. When we got to where the highway crosses the Obion River, we lost his trail in the swamp out by the printing plant. It was like he vanished into thin air."

"Or into the swamp," Deputy King adds.

CHAPTER NINE

Not the swamp!" Ella cries.

"Every fork of that damned river is cursed," Carter angrily spits out each word.

April's soft crying drifts across the group like a chilling fog.

Sheriff Ron Harris clears his throat. "Well, look, there's nothing else to do tonight. I need to get back to town and put together a search party for the morning. We'll get the rescue squad to bring their boats out to the swamp. I'll also call the TBI and FBI to see if they will help."

Turning to Bubba, he says, "Bubba, thanks for bringing your dogs out here. They were a big help. At least we have some sense of what direction to look tomorrow.

"Deputy, let's go. You drive."

Deputy King quickly makes his way to the patrol car and slides behind the steering wheel. When he starts the engine the bright headlights cause the rest of the group to squint and cover their eyes. After the sheriff's car drives away, the group stares in silence at the retreating taillights.

Bubba Garrett bends down and picks up the leash to his sleeping bloodhounds. "Wake up, you two. Time to go home."

He pauses for a moment, then looks at Tucker. "I'm sure sorry we didn't find March. My dogs don't usually lose a trail like that. I can't figure it out."

"Thankye fer tryin', Bubba," Tucker replies. "I'm sure y' done yore best."

The tailgate of his pickup truck bangs loudly as Bubba releases the catch. Instead of jumping into the bed of the truck, his tired hounds sit at his feet looking like a pile of wrinkled raincoats. Bubba bends down and wraps each of them in an arm. "Bless your hearts. Ya'll is worn out. Let me help you in. We're headed home."

As Bubba drives off, Carter says, "Is there anything I can do here, Tucker?"

"Don't know what it'd be," Tucker replies.

"Then I'm going to head home, too. August, you coming?"

August resolutely walks to the porch steps and perches on the top step. "I'm staying the night with Tucker."

Carter looks to Tucker who gives an affirmative nod.

"That sounds good," Carter says. "I'll be back around in the morning."

The springs of the tractor seat complain loudly as he settles his large frame on the seat.

As Carter cranks up his tractor, Ella says to Tucker, "Let me help you take all these jars back inside."

"Y' ain't gotta do that. I can manage."

Jars in hand, Ella walks past Tucker and says, "I can help if I want to." She opens the screen door and disappears inside.

Tucker joins her in the kitchen, fills the sink with water, and sets about cleaning up the few dishes that are on the counter. As Tucker bends over to put her cast-iron skillet away in the oven, Ella sees the torn edge of an envelope sticking out of her back pocket. Remembering the postman's visit to her porch with the registered letter yesterday, her curiosity is piqued.

Knowing Tucker's penchant for bristling at nosiness, Ella tip-toes into the conversation. "You've had a hard day, haven't you?"

"Jes' been another day, that's all," Tucker replies. Leaning back against the stove, she folds her arms across her chest. "I done decided a long time ago that a day ain't nothin' more than that; good 'r bad, it's jes' a day. Anybody can git through one day. An' I've jes' 'bout made it through this day."

Ella looks thoughtfully at Tucker. "That's what I love about you, Tucker. You can sometimes put things so plain and simple. You strip things down and make them uncomplicated. I, on the other hand, can often make things overly complicated."

"I ain't sure what all that means, but I think I'm s'posed t' say thankye."

Ella laughs. "Yes, it was a compliment. And you're welcome."

The women turn to the dishes at the double sink. Tucker washes the jars and hands them to Ella who rinses and dries them.

After a few moments of silence, Ella says, "Can I ask you about something?"

"Well, sure y' can."

"What was that registered letter about that you got yesterday?"

Tucker's hands freeze in the frothy suds of the dishwater. Softly she says, "I done fergot 'bout that . . ." She slowly begins washing another jar.

Knowing she might be rebuffed, Ella asks, "More bad news?"

Tucker hands her the last jar and pulls the stopper in the sink. "Let's sit at th' table fer a minute."

They pull chairs out and sit facing each other at the table. A sucking sound from the sink echoes through the kitchen as the drain swallows the last of the soapy dishwater.

Tucker pulls the wrinkled envelope out of her hip pocket and lays it on the table between them. Staring at it, Tucker says, "That right there is gonna change ever'thing. It's gonna be the end of me." Pushing the letter toward Ella, she adds, "Read it yoreself."

Frown lines pull at every crease in Ella's face. Remembering the last time Tucker made her read a letter, Ella places her hands in her lap and says, "Why don't you just tell me?"

Tucker sits back in her chair, leaving the letter lying on the table. "Th' story goes way back. My daddy first bought this farm in 1901. It had a hundered acres in it. After my mother run'd off and he disappeared, th' farm passed on t' me. There wasn't no official papers 'r nothin'; it's jes' that I was th' only one left an' no one objected t' me havin' th' farm. I didn't know nothin' 'bout how t' manage money 'cause I never seen none. Nobody'd ever tol' me 'bout property taxes an' sech things, neither.

"I decided t' let th' Taylor boys rent m' farm ground an' pay me fer it. That helped buy groceries fer me 'n Maisy, buy some feed fer th' animals, things like that.

"Well, when I's 'bout twenty years old, this man come t' m' house with th' sheriff. Said he was th' tax assessor an' th' property taxes ain't been paid in five years. Said they's gonna sell m' farm t' pay m' taxes unless I come up with th' money in ninety days. I said t' 'im, 'Th' hell y' are.' That's when th' sheriff spoke up an' said they could do exactly that.

"I didn't have that kind o' money. So I asked Smiley Carter what I should do."

At the mention of Smiley Carter's name Ella's eyes brighten and she smiles. "So you've always trusted Smiley? He's an honest man?"

Tucker cocks her head at the questions. "Well, o' course 'e is. In spite o' what 'im an' Maisy done, he's a good man."

"So what did Smiley tell you to do?"

"He said I should talk t' th' Taylor boys an' see if they might want t' buy enough o' my land t' pay th' taxes. He said he knowed lots of folks what done that.

"So that's what I did an' they was glad I offered. Said they'd buy th' whole farm if I'd sell it. But I said no, I jes' wanted t' sell enough t' be able t' keep that man from taken th' farm from me.

"An' that's the way it's been ever since then."

Ella realizes that Tucker considers her explanation complete. Ella asks, "What do you mean, 'That's the way it's been ever since'?"

"I mean ever' four 'r five years I have t' sell off a piece t' pay m' taxes an' be able to keep th' rest. An' that's where th' problem is."

Sitting forward in her chair, Tucker places her forearms on the table and folds her hands. Dropping her head she says, "It's time t' pay again an' I ain't got no more land t' sell."

Tucker's words fall onto Ella like a shattered chandelier. It's as if she feels pinpricks all over her body. "No more land and no money?" she says softly.

Tucker raises her head and looks at Ella. "I know what people 'round here think. I'm th' Welfare Queen. I got it made livin' off th' government. I'm on a gravy train." The tops of her cheeks redden. "Well, I'll tell y' what a life livin' on welfare is like. Look 'round y'." She sweeps her arm across the room. "This look like I got it easy? Them grandkids never had more than two pair o' jeans at a time their whole life. They's many a day I sent 'em t' school an' then cried 'cause they didn't have no nice clothes t' wear. An' it was my garden and animals help us have decent food, not welfare."

As her bottom lip begins trembling, she jerks a handkerchief out of her hip pocket and blows her nose loudly. Wiping her eyes she says, "Welfare is a gravy train? That's a joke! All I got left is th' two 'r three acres where m' house an' barn sit an' where I got m' garden spot."

Ella's been holding her breath throughout Tucker's heartfelt explanation. She slowly exhales and takes in a fresh breath. "How long do you have to get the taxes paid?"

Tucker picks up the fateful letter and waves it. "This here's th' first warnin'. I'll ignore it an' they'll send others. I'll make a promise 'r two I can't keep, jes' t' keep 'em at bay. My guess is in six t' nine months, this place won't no longer be mine."

CHAPTER TEN

Smiley Carter leans back against the wagon hitched to his tractor. Squinting at the afternoon sun, he takes a bandanna out of his hip pocket and swipes his face from his forehead down to his chin, then wipes the back of his neck.

"Ol' sun, you are having a hard time letting go of summer, ain't you? But you can't hold on forever. October's done arrived and your hold on this part of the earth is slipping away."

Turning to face the wagon, he reaches into the corner for a thermos. Twisting open the top, he pours the cold water into the lid. He gulps it down in two swallows.

"Ahhh, mighty fine, mighty fine," he says.

After he returns the thermos to its corner, Carter surveys his field. Trees in brilliant fall colors create a beautiful frame around the field—the brass of the hickories, red of the sweet gums, burgundy of the sumac, yellow maples, burnt-orange elms, rust-colored sycamores. Peeking through the grass in the field are scores of orange pumpkins. Their placement in the field looks as if the giant from *Jack and the Beanstalk* dropped some seeds that floated down like dandelion fluff, briefly grabbing hold, then letting go of the slightest breeze.

Some of the pumpkins are healthier and larger than others. They range in size from those that would fit in a gallon bucket to a few that would have difficulty squeezing into a number two washtub.

Carter walks over to one of the largest pumpkins. Bending over and smiling, he pats it like he would his pet rat terrier, Susie. "Ain't you a fine-looking pumpkin? Somebody's going to be mighty excited to take you home."

Squatting down, he wraps his arms around the pumpkin and stands up with a grunt. Taking small, careful steps, he walks to the rear of the wagon and gently lays his prize pumpkin down.

"Whew!" he exclaims. "You is one heavy pumpkin!"

A distant rumbling catches Carter's attention. He turns to face the road. In the distance he sees the afternoon school bus bouncing and weaving over the uneven gravel road. He waits with anticipation to see if the bus will slow as it approaches his house. He hopes that August will get off and stay the night with him.

In the two months since March's disappearance, August's stays with him have become infrequent. "I feel bad for Tucker being all alone," August has told him more than once.

Carter smiles as he hears the squeal of the bus's brakes. The bus stops and its door opens with a bang. August's lean, lithe body is expelled from the bus, looking to Carter like August has been picked up by two cowboys in a saloon and tossed through the swinging doors onto the dusty street outside. Landing on the balls of his feet, August spins around to face the bus.

He raises his clenched fists in the air and raises both middle fingers. Carter can tell August is yelling something to the kids on the bus, but Carter can't distinguish the words.

As the bus pulls away, August picks up a rock and flings it at its dust-covered rear window.

When August turns to walk toward the house, Carter can see the boy's torn shirt. "August," he calls out. Waving his hand, he yells, "Over here in the field."

August stops and turns toward the sound of Carter's voice.

"I sure could use some help," Carter says.

August walks stiffly toward his father. Instead of using the open gate a few feet away, he slips between two strands of the barbed wire fence that wraps around the field. As August gets closer Carter takes in more details of the boy's appearance. One knee of his jeans has a corner tear. The knuckles of one hand have an abrasion. There is dried blood at the corner of his mouth. One eye is swollen and half-closed. His bottom lip is puffy.

August comes to a stop four feet from Carter. They stare at each other for a moment.

"Looks like you had an interesting day today," Carter says.

"Yeah, I guess," August replies.

Carter turns to the pile of pumpkins in the half-filled trailer. "I wish you'd look at this pile of pumpkins. Don't that look nice? And look at this big giant one. It may be the biggest I ever raised."

August steps closer to examine the cargo. His good eye widens. "Wow! That thing is huge!"

Relieved that the boy is willing to talk, Carter says, "We gonna make some nice money selling these to stores and people around here. And remember, half of the money is yours, just like I told you. You helped raise them."

But just as quickly as August engaged with Carter, his mood shifts and he stares into the distance, ignoring the promise of money.

Carter turns and walks toward a pumpkin hiding in the grass. Grasshoppers jump away at his approach. With his back to August he says, "You want to help me load the rest of these?"

The glazed look in August's eyes evaporates and he focuses again on Carter. Walking toward him, August says, "Sure."

The two work in silence as they gather the pumpkins close to the wagon and tractor.

Eventually, Carter says, "I'm going to pull the tractor forward a bit. No use in walking any farther than we have to."

He eases the tractor forward twenty yards. As he gets off, he says, "You want a drink of water? I've got some in a thermos here in the trailer."

August walks toward a pumpkin and says, "No, thanks."

"Well, I believe I need one."

As August approaches the wagon carrying a pumpkin, Carter finishes his cup of water. Without looking directly at August, Carter asks, "You want to talk about what happened?"

"It wasn't nothing," August replies as he lifts the pumpkin onto the wagon.

"Hmmm . . . I'm not sure your eye and lip would agree with you on that. Wonder what they'd say if they could talk? They might say, 'Well, Mr. Carter, it's like this. We was minding our own business when suddenly there come this flying fist and since we wasn't expecting it, we didn't duck to get out of the way. Yes, sir, that's what happened.'"

In spite of his dark mood August smiles. But just as quickly as a breath disappears in the frosty air of winter, August's smile evaporates and a scowl takes its place. "It's that Hartsfeld kid again," he says.

"The family that moved down here from Chicago?" Carter asks.

"That's him," August replies.

"Let's talk and work. Sometimes words come easier when you're busy doing something." Carter walks toward an especially large pumpkin. "Come help me with this one and tell me what happened."

CHAPTER ELEVEN

Thankful for an outlet for his anxious energy, August joins Carter on the opposite side of the pumpkin.

"He called me a nigger and said my mama was a whore." The words escape in a rush as if he were vomiting them out.

"Hmph," Carter grunts. "I see. Them's pretty strong words." He reaches down and pulls slack into his pant legs. "Remember to bend your knees when you pick up," he advises.

They squat beside the pumpkin and reach underneath the bottom.

"You ready?" Carter asks.

"Yep."

"On three. One . . . two . . . three."

They stand at the same time, cradling the pumpkin between them. As they walk sideways to the trailer, Carter asks, "Wonder why that Hartsfeld kid called you a nigger? I mean, I wonder what he meant by it? Now be careful setting this pumpkin in the trailer. I don't want it to fall off and bust."

Once the pumpkin is safely in its temporary home, they rest their arms on the bed of the trailer.

"I don't care what he meant by it," August says. "I don't like it. And anybody who calls me that is asking for trouble."

"That's a Yankee for you," Carter says. "They're all a bunch of worthless carpetbaggers with smart-aleck mouths and attitudes. I wish somebody'd just kill all of them."

Mouth agape, August stares at Carter. "But that's not true. Our basketball coach moved here from Michigan and he's cool. Everybody likes him."

"Oh, yeah, that's right. I forgot about him. But he's the only one. The world would be better off without the rest of them Yankees."

Carter walks away to retrieve another pumpkin.

August looks at him thoughtfully, confusion etched on his face. He's never heard his father speak ill of anyone, except maybe Judge Jack.

Carter approaches the wagon holding a small pumpkin by its green stem. "What are you looking at?" he asks. "You got a problem with anything I said?"

"Well, I was thinking that coach's wife and kids came from Michigan, too, and they're probably decent like he is. And maybe their parents were good people, too."

Carter rubs his chin thoughtfully. "I guess that's possible— maybe. Maybe you're right. Maybe they're not all bad like when I was growin' up." He pauses. "What does the word 'nigger' mean?"

"It's what people used to call black folks, like when you were growing up. And that's what they called slaves, too. Right?"

"That's true." Carter walks away again into the field of waiting pumpkins. Over his shoulder he says, "Are you black?"

August is stunned by the question. It's the question he's asked himself often but never spoken aloud. "Am I black?" he repeats. "I'd say half of me is, isn't it?"

Approaching the wagon carrying two more pumpkins, Carter says, "That's not for me to decide. That's up to you." He faces August. "Are you a slave?"

August's fists clench. "No! That's a stupid question."

"So why did that Taylor kid call you a nigger?"

"He thinks he's better than I am just because he's white and I'm black."

Carter reaches in the wagon to retrieve his thermos. "I'd say your answer is half right." He pauses to drink directly from the mouth of the thermos. He holds it toward August, who shakes his head.

"What do you mean, 'half right'?" August asks.

Carter heads back into the field. "Are you going to help me finish getting these pumpkins? Or are you just going to talk? I never saw a boy so eager to talk."

August joins Carter and walks beside him. He has had a growth spurt over the summer, and his long legs now allow him to walk in perfect stride with the older man.

"The Hartsfeld boy does think he's better than you. That's for certain," Carter says. "But that's because of what he's been taught—that black people are less than human, one step above apes. He's racist."

Bending over to cut a pumpkin loose from its vine, he continues, "Always remember, August, that no one is born racist. They have to be taught it, usually by their family. Those things I said about Yankees a while ago, I don't believe a word of it. But I wanted you to hear what prejudice sounds like and where it comes from. It comes from a heart darkened by fear and anger. That's what I learned from Martin Luther King."

August's mouth pops open. "You knew Martin Luther King?"

"It's not like we was good friends," Carter replies, "but I did meet him the time he was in Memphis. The same weekend he got killed. Plus, I listened to his speeches on the radio and television.

"Be proud of who you are because color has nothing to do with the quality of a person's life. That's what I learned from him. No one can take that away from you.

"I've never told you this, but my granddaddy was a slave. Which means your great-granddaddy was a slave. But you know what? I'm not ashamed of that. I'm proud that he survived it without turning into an angry, bitter man.

"Now pick up those two pumpkins over there. We're nearly done."

August walks slowly toward the pumpkins, trying to digest everything Carter has told him. He rejoins Carter at the wagon and adds his two pumpkins to the harvest.

"That's a pretty picture right there," Carter says, admiring the pile of pumpkins. Looking at August, he says, "Is that why you got into a fight? Because he called you a nigger and what he said about your mother?"

August shakes his head. "No, sir. I ignored him when he said that."

Surprised, Carter asks, "Then what triggered the fight."

Through clenched teeth, August says, "When he said March disappeared because Tucker killed him, chopped him up, and scattered the pieces in the Obion River bottom."

CHAPTER TWELVE

Stepping out of the shower, Ella towels herself dry. She stands in front of the mirror and rubs the fog off its surface until she can see clearly. Her towel falls heavily to the floor. She pushes it aside with her foot.

Gazing at her reflection, she uses both index fingers to gently touch the pink scars on her chest where her breasts used to be. Her fingers trace the horizontal trails left by the surgeon's scalpel.

Her gaze shifts from her reflection in the mirror, and she looks down at her flat chest, which is accentuated by the natural curve of her abdomen. Speaking to her abdomen, she says, "There was a time when I couldn't see you because you lived in the shadow of my breasts." Her voice catches.

Ella looks back at the mirror. She slowly runs her hand over her head. Feeling the prickliness of hair returning, she opens the cabinet and takes out a bottle of lotion and a safety razor.

She opens the lotion bottle and takes a slow sniff. The coconut aroma triggers memories of the ocean, suntan lotion, sand, and warm breezes. She pours some lotion in the palm of her hand and rubs it on her scalp. Then she carefully pulls the razor through the soft liquid, leaving in its wake gleaming patches of slick skin.

Once Ella is finished, she rinses her head, dries it, and goes out into the hall. Turning to the linen closet, she opens the door and scans a shelf with scores of colorful silk scarves lying folded in rows. She chooses a paisley print with coneflower blue, daffodil yellow, and touches of red. With the practiced moves and deftness of a magician, she wraps the scarf around her head.

Glancing at the clock, she sees it is eight thirty. After dabbing on a bit of lipstick, she exits the bathroom and goes to her bedroom where she finishes dressing.

When she goes into the kitchen Ella looks out the window of the back door toward Mansfield Road. After a few minutes she sees Smiley Carter coming over the hill on his tractor. Smiling, Ella takes two coffee cups and one saucer from the cabinet and sets them on her kitchen table. She takes the aluminum foil off of a partially eaten apple pie, cuts two pieces, and places them on plates. When she hears the sound of the approaching tractor, she goes to her front porch to greet him.

Carter coasts the final twenty yards and when the tractor rolls to a stop, he cuts off the engine. He smiles broadly. "Good morning, Ella."

"Good morning, Irvin," Ella responds.

Carter freezes halfway to the ground. He looks at her with an uncharacteristic frown. "You know I don't like you to call me that."

Walking out to the tractor, Ella smiles warmly. "But I love it. It's your name. For the longest time I thought Smiley was your given name."

Carter steps to the ground with a grunt. "And I don't know why in the world I done told you my real name. That was a mistake for sure."

She takes his large hand between hers and says, "Your secret is safe with me. I haven't even told Tucker. Besides it's a famous name now that that basketball player is so famous."

Following her pull toward the house, Carter says, "Yeah, but even he doesn't go by his given name. People call him Magic."

"One thing you two have in common, though," Ella says as she opens the front door, "is that beautiful smile!"

In the kitchen Carter peels off his denim jumper and hangs it on the back of a chair, then takes off his cap revealing his white, close-cropped hair. Sitting down, he eyes the pie and says, "Mmmm-mmmm, now that looks fine. You sure does know how to make some fine pie."

Ella pours the coffee in their cups, returns the pot to the stove, and settles into her chair. She watches Carter's familiar habit of pouring his coffee into the saucer. As he blows and takes a sip, she asks, "Where did you learn how to drink coffee like that?"

Carter lowers the saucer until he can see Ella. Setting it down on the table, Carter replies, "The first person I saw do it was Mama Mattie. Some of us kids would be over at her house and would peek through the window while our folks was talking. When she did it, it made her look elegant and smart. Mama Mattie was a legend when I was growing up. Imitating her was considered a way to set yourself apart.

"I know now that it ain't good manners, but I've done this way for so long I don't know no other way."

Sensing that she has perhaps embarrassed Carter, Ella says, "I find it fascinating. You're the only person I've ever seen do it. That's the only reason I was asking. Why don't I try it?"

She gets up quickly and goes to the cabinets. Reaching up to open the door, she sways and grabs the edge of the counter with both hands to steady herself. All the light around her seems to dim. She shakes her head and the light returns.

Ella glances over her shoulder to see if Carter has noticed. She is grateful that he is focused on pouring more coffee into his saucer.

Returning to her chair, she tips her cup until coffee begins to dribble over the side and splashes into her saucer.

"You'll learn," Carter says, as he watches her with amusement, "that you need to hold your cup closer to the saucer so it doesn't splash onto the table."

Ella eyes her saucer as she would a puzzle. She looks at Carter.

"Pinch the edge with your thumb and finger on both sides, thumbs on top," he says, demonstrating as he speaks.

Mirroring his movements, Ella slowly raises the saucer to her lips. Tipping it toward her, she makes a loud slurping sound and coffee dribbles down her chin and neck. "Ow!" she cries as she drops the saucer to the table.

Carter jumps up and grabs the washcloth hanging on the faucet and rushes to her side. He dabs her mouth and neck carefully. "Are you okay, Ella?"

"Yes, yes, I'm fine," she says. "I think it scared me more than it burned me."

As Carter sits back down, he looks at her and puts his hand over his mouth. But his hand can't conceal that his eyes are dancing with laughter.

"What?" Ella says, smiling.

Bursting into laughter, Carter says, "I believe that was the loudest slurp I ever heard. It sounded like a kid trying to get the last drops of soda with a straw."

Feigning indignation, Ella says, "Well, I never!" But her laughter cannot be contained, either. The sound of their laughter, her brilliant tenor and Carter's rich baritone, causes her Autoharp to resonate even though it is in its case.

Carter stamps his foot and slaps his knee as laughter rolls freely from him. "And I don't think you even got any coffee in your mouth!"

Ella laughs so hard that she begins to cough. Her eyes redden with the effort to catch her breath. She holds the washcloth over her mouth. Finally, she is able to contain the coughing and breathe more easily.

She dabs her tears as Carter's laughter subsides, too.

As they look at each other, an unexpected seriousness fills the distance between them, catching them both off guard.

"You know," Ella says thoughtfully, "my move out here to this McDaniel house has brought me more joys than I could have ever dreamed. I thought my life was over when I moved out here. I viewed this house as my mausoleum."

Carter fixes his eyes on hers.

"And then," Ella continues, "I met Tucker." She laughs. "Tucker. What an unusual woman. One of the most amazing women I've ever known. And, of course the kids, especially April." Her eyes tear again.

Carter clears his throat. "And you's the best thing that ever happened to this neck of the woods. I don't know where Tucker'd be if it wasn't for you."

Shaking his head, he continues, "It's been two months since little March done disappeared. And ain't nobody seen or heard nothing. That's sad, just plain sad. I don't know why Tucker ain't outta her mind."

Ella smiles. "Tucker doesn't see the world and time like most folks do. It's something I've tried to learn from her. She says nothing matters but this moment right here, right now. She says she focuses on one slice of time at a time. Getting stuck on the past will weigh you down and looking into the future will only create worries."

"I think if it weren't for that philosophy, Tucker would be locked up somewhere, in prison or at Western State Hospital. She's never had anything come easy."

Looking directly at Carter, she says, "And that, Irvin Smiley Carter, is why I can enjoy being friends with you."

In spite of his best efforts to frown, Carter's trademark smile breaks through. He slides his hand, palm down, across the table toward her.

Ella's hand meets his halfway. Sliding her thin fingers in between his, she looks down and says, "It looks like the keys on a piano. What would Judge Jack say if he could see me now?"

They have been so focused on their conversation that neither has heard the car pull up in front of Ella's house or the car door closing as the driver exits. The sudden rapping on her front door startles them both.

CHAPTER THIRTEEN

Eyes wide, Ella says, "I wonder who that could be? You stay here and I'll go check."

Smiley Carter looks at her with concern and starts to get up. "Are you sure?"

Motioning him to stay, she says, "Yes, yes. I'll be fine."

Forgoing her usual habit of glancing out the window before opening her front door, Ella walks straight to the door and pulls it open. Not immediately recognizing the person at her door, she looks past him and sees a familiar white Lincoln Continental in the driveway. She frowns and looks back to the figure at her door.

Judge Jack. She scans him, her eyes sharp as an eagle's, and she realizes why he was difficult to recognize at first. His hair, normally neatly combed, is tousled; his eyes are bloodshot and have heavy bags under them; he looks like he hasn't shaved in four or five days, his cheeks dotted with small scabs. His white shirt is stained and rumpled, and his loose shoelaces trail down like red worms looking to escape back into the dark ground. Ella's head jerks back involuntarily when the smell of body odor mixed with whiskey strikes her nostrils.

Judge Jack notices her flinch and makes an effort to straighten from his slightly stooped position. Tucking his shirt more tightly into his pants and pushing one hand through his tangled hair, he says, "Hello, Ella. It's been a while."

"It's been a pleasant two years since I've seen you," Ella says.

"Well, yes, I guess it has been. I tend to lose track of time since I've retired."

There is a hesitancy and uncertainty in Judge Jack that she's never seen before. But she knows to be wary just the same. "What brings you out here?"

"Are you not going to ask me in? There is something I want to ask you about. It's about April."

At the mention of her granddaughter's name, Ella's heart beats faster. Alarms go off in her head. But she manages to keep her voice calm. "Then why don't you come in?" She steps aside to allow him entrance.

Judge Jack warily peers inside before walking through the door.

Ella closes the door behind him. When she turns around, the Judge is standing in the middle of her living room. Ten feet away, Smiley Carter stands facing him.

Carter's normally pleasant expression has been supplanted by a malevolent look. A chill runs down Ella's spine at this heretofore unseen side of her friend.

Turning to Ella, the Judge snaps, "What's he doing here?"

Folding her arms across her chest, Ella replies, "First of all, you don't come into my house and question me about anything that is going on in it. I'll have here who I want and I'll do what I want and you don't have any say-so about it. Is that clear? Because if it's not, you can turn around, get back in your car, and go back to whatever rock you crawled out from under."

Judge Jack is caught off guard by Ella's assertiveness. He tries to gather himself with a comeback, but the battle has been won before it started. "Yes . . . yes, you're right, Ella," he says meekly. "I have no right. I apologize."

Looking at Smiley Carter, he adds, "And I apologize to you, Carter."

Ella takes a slow, quiet breath and exhales. Lowering her arms to her sides, she says, "So, what brings you out here?"

Judge Jack teeters a bit to one side but catches his balance. "Is it okay if we sit down and talk? I seem to be having a bit of difficulty standing for long periods of time."

A fleeting look of concern passes across Ella's face. "I suppose it'll be all right. Why don't you sit in the chair? Smiley, would you mind bringing us all a cup of coffee?"

Satisfied that the Judge is not an immediate threat, Carter says, "Sure thing. I'll have it right up. How do you like yours, Judge?"

Without thinking, Ella says, "He likes it with two spoons of sugar." Flustered that she has responded instinctively from old memories, she frowns.

Judge Jack smiles. "You still remember."

Ella notices that his smile is a bit askew, no doubt the result of Tucker permanently rearranging his jawline with her axe handle more than two years ago.

"When's the last time you saw our son, Cade?" the Judge asks.

"I know I have a biological son, but I haven't had a true son in a long, long time," Ella replies. "You robbed him of character, you know."

The Judge looks at his folded hands in his lap. "You know he's on death row, don't you?"

"I'm aware of that."

"We're still working on filing appeals. I'm hopeful something will save him."

He raises his head. They lock eyes. Ella says, "Only God can save Cade."

Just then, Carter walks in carrying three cups of coffee. He lets the Judge take one and then sits beside Ella on the couch, offering her one of the remaining cups.

Judge Jack's hand trembles as he lifts the coffee to his lips. He takes a long sip. Closing his eyes, he says, "That's a good cup of coffee."

Suddenly there are two hard raps on the front door. Before anyone reacts, it swings open and Tucker steps inside, brandishing an axe handle.

Judge Jack's coffee cup shatters on the floor.

"Is ever'thing all right?" Tucker asks.

Ella hands her cup to Carter and rises from the couch. "Yes, yes, Tucker. We're all fine. No problems. Come right in. Grab a kitchen chair and bring it in here."

As Tucker strides past the Judge, he tucks his feet under his chair as far as he can and pushes himself deeply into its padding. Tucker doesn't even glance at him.

She returns to the living room and sits in her chair, the axe handle across her thighs.

Comfortable that her friend isn't going to resort to violence, Ella sits back down and takes her cup from Carter.

An awkward silence fills the room.

Raising her eyebrows, Ella looks at the Judge and says, "Are you going to tell me what brought you out here?"

The Judge glances around the room. "Well, I didn't expect to have an audience."

If he expected that his comment would trigger an "Excuse me, I'll leave" from either Carter or Tucker, his hopes were dashed by their stony silence.

Clearing his throat, he says, "I came to discuss our granddaughter, April."

CHAPTER FOURTEEN

At Judge Jack's words about April, Tucker grips her axe handle.

Carter chokes and coughs as he tries to swallow a mouthful of coffee.

Ella feels a chill run down her spine. Making an effort to keep her voice calm, she says, "What's on your mind about April?"

The Judge stands up beside his chair and rests his hand on the back of it to steady himself. He reaches for the lapel of his jacket, but grasps empty air. He looks down dumbly, puzzled that his jacket isn't there. In an attempt to cover his gaffe he raises his hand to his mouth and coughs loudly.

"It was a shocking revelation," he begins, "when I learned that I had a granddaughter. But it was a revelation that warmed my heart. Especially when I learned it was the lovely April.

"Recently, it occurred to me that I really don't know the child and she doesn't know me. That is my fault. I haven't reached out to her like I should. I'm now eager to remedy that situation."

He scans the faces of his audience, trying to read them as he used to read juries. He misjudges their stunned silence as mute agreement with his sentiments. Emboldened by his misconception, he warms to his message and begins slowly pacing, hands folded behind his back.

"So the question is," he says, "what is the best way for April to get to know her grandfather? You may not know this, but I am single again. It's only me and my housekeeper rattling around in my big old house. There is more than enough room for April to come and live with me."

Tucker's angry voice cuts the air like a knife. "The hell you say!" She starts to get out of her chair, but her knees buckle and she sits back heavily.

Judge Jack moves as quickly as his unsteady steps will allow and positions himself so that his chair is between him and Tucker.

Ella's face turns as white as a dogwood bloom. "Jack, you can't be serious. She doesn't even know you and you expect her to come live with you? She would be scared to death. You can't possibly believe that anyone here would allow that to happen."

Unfazed by his ex-wife's response, Judge Jack says, "Actually, I expected that would be your reaction. And I can see the wisdom in what you say. That is why I have an additional offer."

Like a maestro at the podium, Judge Jack has seized their attention. He holds the silence, letting the tension build and beg for release. And just when the long silence seems to indicate the song may have come to an end, he delivers a dramatic downbeat.

"Ella, I want you to marry me. I now realize that our divorce was the biggest mistake of my life. I treated you badly our entire marriage, and I apologize for that. I want you to come home, home to the material comforts of the life we once had together."

Tucker feels like she's been kicked in the chest by a horse. The Judge's words trigger an old feeling, a feeling she hasn't felt since she was a child: terror. She feels a choking sensation and has difficulty breathing. Staring in disbelief at Judge Jack, she sees in his face, just for a moment, the leering face of her long-dead father. She shakes her head, trying to clear her vision.

Smiley Carter sags back onto the couch. A familiar feeling of helplessness pours over him. He feels a sharp pain in his chest, as if someone has viciously plunged a dagger into his heart.

The room swims before Ella's eyes. She finds it impossible to focus her vision. Like snapshots from a photo album, images flash through her mind—young Cade sliding down the banister, her formal dining room filled with guests in gowns and tuxedos, the opulent furniture of her massive master bedroom. She sees herself reflected in the full-length mirror; she is wearing a teal-colored evening gown with a heavily jeweled necklace around her neck, and her long hair cascades to her shoulders.

Ella feels as if she has fallen off a cliff and is holding her breath until she crashes on the rocks below. But then she looks at Tucker and strength fills her chest. Her vision clears and she looks at Judge Jack and sees the hollow shell of a man that he has become. With sudden clarity she realizes that what she sees on his outside is but a manifestation of what he always was on the inside.

She surprises herself with the ease with which her voice comes. "No, Jack. My life here has been filled with more contentment than I had in all my years of living with you."

Judge Jack's face turns crimson. "What is the matter with you? You live out here in this tiny house that looks like a stiff wind would collapse it, with this white trash and this nigger as your so-called friends. You can never offer April what a life with me would afford her. If you come to live with me, you won't have a care in the world."

So intent is Judge Jack in his argument that he fails to see the rising color in Ella's cheeks. He is caught off guard when she springs from the couch.

In two quick steps she is in front of him. Then, with the strength that comes from years of pent-up resentment and anger, Ella slaps him so hard that he is driven to his knees.

Looking down at his kneeling form, Ella says, "You listen to me, Jack McDade. What I have found living out here is something you will never understand because you have never known it. It is people who respect me for who I am, not because of the power that I have. Respect that comes at the price of power will exist only as long as the power stays in place. Once it's gone, the respect evaporates like dew in the morning sun.

"What I can give April or, what I should say is, what *we* can give April"—she gives a sweep of her hand toward Tucker and Carter— "is a life of appreciation for small blessings. She already has learned the value of hard work. She will lose that if she lives with you.

"A privileged life, the kind of life that you and I grew up with and had together, is a dangerous path. It's easy to fall into the temptation of judging others who are less fortunate and seeing them as less than, seeing them as lazy, seeing them as two-dimensional caricatures.

"But let me tell you something. The people I have met out here have more depth of character than the deepest well, more facets than the finest cut diamond, and more determination and grit than . . . than . . ." She searches for the right description. Then, smiling, she says, ". . . than a coonhound hot on the trail."

Having gained the upper hand, Ella says, "Get out of my house, Jack McDade! And don't ever come back here again!"

Judge Jack staggers to his feet like a wounded buffalo. Rubbing the side of his face where already the red handprint of Ella's forceful slap is beginning to show, he says, "Don't think this is the end of it. I still know people. I'm still a force to be reckoned with."

At this, Tucker rises slowly from her chair. Walking deliberately toward him, she draws back her axe handle like a baseball bat and says calmly, "I'll show you some force."

Judge Jack's eyes widen and he cries out. He quickly makes his way to the front door and stumbles onto the porch, leaving the door open behind him.

Ella goes to the window and watches him as he drives off.

Suddenly she grips the curtains. She sways for a moment, then closes her eyes and collapses to the floor. Pulling the curtains from their clips on the rod as she falls, they float down and cover her body like a shroud.

CHAPTER FIFTEEN

Ella!" Carter and Tucker cry out.

Carter jumps off the couch and rushes to Ella's side. Kneeling, he pulls the curtains off her to reveal her pale face.

"Please, Lord," Tucker says in a whisper, "don't let her be dead."

Carter clasps Ella's hand in between his and lifts it. Bowing his head he says, "Lord God above, I know you always knows what's best, but please don't let this be the time that you take this woman from us. Let her stay a bit longer, Lord. There are folks here that still need her. "

"Foolish man," Ella's voice comes quietly from the floor, "I'm not dead and I'm not dying. I think I just fainted."

Carter's eyes pop open. "Blessed Jesus! Thank you, blessed Jesus!"

Ella tries to push herself off the floor but she is unable to brace herself and falls back.

"Help th' woman up," Tucker exclaims. "She's gonna bust 'er head open waitin' on you t' help 'er. Save yore prayin' 'til we see t' 'er. Lay 'er on th' couch an' I'll fetch a glass o' water an' a cool wash rag."

Carter helps Ella to a sitting position, then slips his hands under her arms and lifts her to a standing position.

Her rubbery legs cause Ella to throw her arms around him to keep from falling back down.

Carter bends and sweeps her legs from under her with one arm and cradles her torso to him with the other. He walks to the couch and as carefully as if he were carrying young April, he lays her on the couch. Carefully, he eases a pillow under her head. Reaching to the back of the couch, he pulls the decorative afghan down and tucks it around her.

"How's that?" he asks softly.

"Better," she says.

Tucker walks in and motions for Carter to scoot out of the way. Sitting beside Ella, she lifts Ella's head and puts the glass to her mouth. "Take a sip o' this." As Ella swallows, Tucker adds, "It'll put some starch back in yore shorts."

Ella coughs and her cheeks redden. "What in the world is that? I feel it burning all the way to my toes."

Cautiously, Carter says, "Tucker . . . you didn't, did you?"

Looking innocent, Tucker says, "What 'r y' talkin' 'bout? It's jes' some cough medicine I carry with me fer 'mergencies jes' like this."

She forces the rim between Ella's lips and tilts the glass up. "Take another sip. It's helpin' already. Look at that color in 'er cheeks!"

Ella coughs again and grabs Tucker's wrist to push the glass away.

"Oh my Lord, Tucker," Carter says. "You gonna kill the woman. She's needing to catch her breath and you're boiling it out of her."

"Whew!" Ella exclaims as she pushes the afghan off. "Let me sit up. I'm getting hot."

Smiling triumphantly, Tucker says, "That's a gal. Here, y' hold on t' this. Y' might need it." And she presses the damp washcloth into her hand.

Ella takes a deep breath and blows it out loudly. "I am feeling better." Looking at Tucker in amazement, she says, "Maybe you need to give me a bottle of that cough medicine." Laughing, she adds, "A *small* bottle."

Carter sits down beside Ella on the couch and takes out his bandanna. Wiping sweat from his face, he says, "Woman, you 'bout scared us both to death. I thought you'd done died!"

"Oh, I'm a long way from that. I guess that visit was so unexpected and I got so upset." Shaking her head, she says, "What a pitiful sight he was. Have you all ever seen anything so pitiful looking?"

"I heared tell," Carter says, "that the Judge has been drinking hard ever since Cade's trial. Then when he lost the election, he didn't know what to do with himself. Seems like he done lost everything. Must be hard for a man to fall that far."

Carter smiles. "But did you see the look on his face when Tucker come bustin' in the door carrying her 'peacemaker' axe handle? I think the Judge had thoughts about running out the back door."

A slight smile makes the effort to pull up the corners of Tucker's mouth. But gravity wins and her features sag to their normal resting place. "All I knowed was that I seen th' Judge's car in yore drive. I didn't see th' tractor, so I didn't know Carter was here. I thought it best t' come down an' make sure ever'thing was all right.

"The Judge ain't never been nothin' but a bully. An' ever' bully I ever knowed, from m' daddy forward, is yellow through an' through. Once y' call their bluff, they'll crawfish back into th' hole they crawled outta.

"But you, Ella McDade, you take th' cake. When y' come off o' that couch, y' looked ten feet tall. An' I ain't never seen a woman slap a man that hard. It give me chills. I nearly let out a rebel yell."

"I don't know what came over me," Ella says, "or where that came from. I think he fell from shock as much from the force of my blow."

"I don't know about that," Carter chimes in. "From where I sat I'd say you knocked the you-know-what out of him. Did you see the handprint on his face? It was a thing of beauty." Looking at Ella, he says, "I didn't know you could get so riled up. I'll definitely remember that and try not to ever cross you."

His deep, rich laughter echoes through the house. Both women find it impossible to resist its contagious nature. They, too, burst into laughter. It is the release that they all need.

Gasping for breath, Carter says between laughs, "And when Tucker stood up and told the Judge, 'I'll show you some force,' he looked like he done stared the Grim Reaper face-to-face. If he'd had a tail, you couldn't have seen it because it would have been tucked so far between his legs that he'd a been chewin' on it."

Both women grab their sides they are laughing so hard. Tears stream down everyone's face. Ella laughs until she begins coughing. She puts the damp cloth to her mouth until she stops coughing. She glances in it and quickly squeezes it shut in her fist.

Looking from Tucker to Carter, she says, "You know, I don't know what I would have done if you all hadn't been here."

"Oh, pshaw, woman," Tucker says, "looks t' me like you'd a done fine."

"No," Ella insists, "I mean it." Her words catch in her throat. She coughs to clear it. "And I don't know what would have happened to me if I'd never met you all. What I thought was the end of my life turned out to be a brand new beginning to my life. I love you both."

"Tucker," Carter says, "I believe Miss Ella's done gotten a little tipsy on your cough medicine. She's talking out of her head. I believe we better let her lie down and try to sleep it off."

"No doubt," Tucker says, nodding.

They both rise. When Ella starts to get up, Tucker says, "Y' stay right there. We know th' way out. I'll be down later t' check on y'."

When the door closes behind them, Ella opens her fist and unfolds the rag she'd used to stifle her coughing. She stares numbly at the crimson blood splattered in it.

CHAPTER SIXTEEN

Ella turns off the gravel road onto the dirt lane leading to Smiley Carter's house. Both sides of the lane are lined with giant maple trees lush in their Technicolor fall display. She slows to a stop, marveling at the variety and shades of color. The show is backlit by the morning sun and rays of light shoot through the palette like a strobe light as the wind shakes the treetops. Some of the leaves relinquish their hold on the twigs that have given them life for the past six months.

One of the leaves finds its way through the open window of Ella's green Ford Pinto and comes to a rest in her lap. Picking it up, Ella says, "Yes, I understand how you feel. We all get tired of what it takes to hold on. Sometimes you just have to let go, don't you?"

"Are you lost, miss?" The deep voice startles her. Her head jerks in the direction of the man's voice. She sees no one. A smile slowly spreads across her face as recognition dawns on her. "Irvin Carter, where are you hiding?" she calls out.

Thirty feet to her left a movement catches her eye. Carter steps from behind one of the maple trees. He beams as he walks toward the car. He is dressed in a red flannel shirt and navy Dickies pants.

His close-cropped white hair makes him look like he slept outside and frost covered his head.

Approaching Ella's car, he says, "Scared you, didn't I?"

"Not at all," Ella lies. "I don't scare that easily."

Feigning shock, Carter says, "Oh really? I guess that open mouth and wide eyes I saw belonged to somebody else who was in the car with you." Putting his hands on the roof of the car and leaning down, he looks through the window. After scanning the front seat and the backseat, he straightens and rubs his chin. Frowning, he says, "Hmmm, I guess whoever was in there was so scared, they has done took off."

Content to continue their game, Ella looks around the inside of the car. Looking surprised, she says, "Well, I declare. You must be right because she was here just a second ago. I guess she's never heard a voice coming out of the trees that sounds like the voice of God."

Carter bursts into laughter and Ella joins in.

When his laughter subsides, Carter asks, "So what brings you over in this direction this morning?"

"Actually," Ella says, "I've come to see you. I've never seen your place before, and I decided you were never going to invite me, so I thought I would just invite myself."

Carter's eyebrows knit together and furrows appear across his broad forehead. "But what if somebody—"

Ella cuts him off. "So, is it okay if a neighbor visits a neighbor?" Turning so that she faces the steering wheel, she says quietly, "But maybe you're busy this morning. I can come some other time."

"No, no. That's not it. I'm just thinking somebody might see your car over here and . . . well, you know . . . you're, uh . . . and I'm . . ."

Ella reaches for the ignition key and starts her car. "Look, I guess I misunderstood. If you're worried about your reputation . . ."

Suddenly, Carter leans down, reaches inside her car, shuts off the engine, and pulls the key out of the ignition. He unbuttons the pocket on his shirt and drops the key inside. Buttoning the pocket he says, "Let's get something straight here. I'm not concerned about my reputation. It's not worth protecting. But yours is. A white woman visiting a black man's house. There it is. I've said it. This ain't Chicago or New York, where those things probably happen all the time. This here is northwest Tennessee. The schools here might be integrated, but people's hearts and minds are not.

"People seeing my tractor in front of your house could say I'm just there to see about doing an odd job or plowing a garden spot for you. But you being at my house? Well, I just don't want to be the cause of anybody talking bad about you. 'Cause if they did, I might have to do something about it."

Turning to face him, Ella places her hand on top of his hand that rests on the edge of her door. "Listen to me, Irvin. I have lived a cautious life. It's like I have tiptoed through life, not doing things just because I was afraid of what someone would think of me. I've held things in and left them unsaid because I was afraid I might be ridiculed or because the person on the other end might not receive them well, thinking me foolish. But no more. If there's anything I've learned from having cancer and living out here in 'Tucker's World,' it's that life is fragile." Looking intently into his dark eyes, she says, "Do you understand?"

"Yes, I do," Carter replies somberly.

"Speaking your mind," Ella continues, "is a very freeing thing. Being open and honest with yourself and with others keeps you from having to look over your shoulder. You just put it out there and people can do what they want to with it—like it or not—it doesn't matter."

A solitary tear escapes from the bottom of Carter's eyelid. It slowly rolls down his cheek, carrying with it his own ache of having lived a cautious life in the rural South. It pauses at the bottom of his chin and then disappears into the folds of his thick neck. He blinks and, like wash water thrown out the back door, his remaining tears splash free and scatter through the air—droplets of shame, anger, fear, and disappointment.

Pulling out his red bandanna from his hip pocket, he wipes his face and blows his nose. Reaching into his shirt pocket he retrieves her car key. He clears his throat and hands it to her. "Excuse my manners, Miss Ella. I'd be pleased to have you visit me. You head on up to the house and go in. I've got to make sure the gate is closed on my pasture. I'll be right along."

CHAPTER SEVENTEEN

Ella stands in front of the modest-sized, redbrick house taking in the details: a shed on one side with a tractor parked inside; on the other side a majestic magnolia tree, its lower branches spreading in a circle thirty feet across and its top reaching close to fifty feet high; white shutters and trim match the mortar between the bricks; potted nandinas with their green and red leaves accessorize the front of the house; two Adirondack chairs and three canebottom chairs sit at comfortable angles on the deep front porch.

She walks up the steps and cautiously opens the front door. Stepping inside, it takes a few moments for her eyes to adjust to the dimmer light. She is struck by how the floor plan resembles the McDaniel house she lives in. She surmises that the same contractor built both houses.

As Ella begins to see the interior more clearly, she is drawn to a wall of framed photographs. There is a grouping of faded sepia tintypes. In one there is a white man sitting on a horse with a black man standing at the front of the horse holding the edge of the bridle bit. In another one there is a black woman surrounded by eleven black children of varying ages. Another shows a black boy and a white boy, both about four years old, dressed alike in white pinafores. Ella's hand covers her mouth as she sees another picture is of a black man hanging by his neck from a tree with five smiling white men posing underneath.

She shifts a few feet to her left and stands before a black-and-white eight by ten of a young man in a military uniform. The familiar smile is missing, but she recognizes the eyes of a young Irvin Carter. Beside it there appears to be a perfect replica of the photograph of the soldier, except this one is in color and is clearly a much more recent photograph. The two faces are identical. To the side of the color photograph is a smaller frame containing numerous medals. Though Ella doesn't know the meaning behind most of them, the Bronze Star jumps out at her. It is exactly like the one her father kept in a plastic case in his desk when she was growing up.

Ella has been so intent on looking at the photographs that she has not heard Carter enter the house. "Enjoying your history lesson?" he says.

Ella spins around. The sudden move destabilizes her, and she throws out her hand to catch herself.

Quick as a cat, Carter springs to her side and grabs her hand. "Easy does it, there," he says.

As the room stops spinning, Ella says, "If you don't quit sneaking up on me, I'm going to . . . well, I'm going to do something." She smiles. "Thanks for catching me."

Turning back to the wall, she says, "These two military photographs. They look like the same person, but I know they can't be. And they both look just like you."

Carter taps the black-and-white photograph. "That there is me. I spent four years in the army during World War II."

Ella waits for an explanation for the color photograph, but Carter falls silent. She looks at him and sees that his features have grown hard. Looking back at the photograph, Ella touches it and says, "This is your son, isn't it?"

Carter nods. "Viet Nam," he says quietly. "He didn't make it."

"I'm so sorry. He must have been an incredibly good soldier. I recognize the Bronze Star."

Carter turns away suddenly and begins walking toward the kitchen. "Would you like some coffee?"

Ella turns and follows his retreating form. "That sounds good. I'm anxious to drink some of your coffee. You're always telling me how weak my coffee is and that yours will put hairs on your chest."

Carter's familiar chuckle reassures her that his dark mood has passed. "I don't know if you're man enough to drink my coffee or not," he says. "Have a seat at the table and I'll put some on."

Ella is amazed at the neatness of his kitchen.

"You want to see how *real* coffee is made?" Carter asks. "Come on over and watch a master."

Ella eagerly joins him.

He turns a gas eye on high. Then he fills a medium-sized pot with hot water from the sink. Sitting it on the flame, he stares into it. "I knows people says a watched pot don't boil, but that ain't so. I want to catch it just before it starts to boil."

After a few moments, tiny air bubbles begin sneaking up the inside of the pot and to the surface. Carter reaches to the cabinet above the stove and retrieves a can of coffee. He scatters three large scoops into the water. He then takes down a small, unlabeled can and adds half a scoop to the pot.

"What was that?" Ella asks.

Giving her a wink, Carter says, "That's the secret ingredient. Learned it from Mama Mattie."

He walks over to the sink and reaches into a coffee cup sitting on the windowsill. He returns to the slowly simmering coffee and opens his closed fist for Ella to see.

"Eggshells?" Ella says in disbelief.

Carter sprinkles them into the pot. "They help hold the grounds down so the coffee is cleaner."

After a few minutes Carter dips the thick, black liquid into their cups. He motions toward the table. "You'd better be sitting down for this," he says with a smile.

"If this is anything like Tucker's special cough medicine, I'm not sure I'm woman enough to drink it," Ella replies, returning his smile.

Lifting his cup toward her, Carter says, "I'll try drinking it like civilized folks instead of using my saucer. To your good health." He tips his cup up and sips loudly. "Ah, now that's a real cup of coffee!"

Ella hesitates, closes her eyes, and takes a sip of the brew. Her eyelids recoil like window shades. Grimacing, she sets the cup down loudly. "Oh my stars, Irvin! I believe that would take paint off a wall. Yeeouch, that's strong. What is that extra ingredient?"

"It's chicory," he says, bemused by her reaction. "One cup will last you all day long."

"I believe you!" Ella exclaims. "If it's all the same to you, I'll take a glass of your homemade cider. Maybe that will take the bitter taste out of my mouth."

Carter retrieves a jar from the refrigerator and pours a glass of honey-colored liquid. He hands it to Ella. He notices her watching him as she is drinking. When she sets the glass down, he says, "Something is on your mind, I can tell. But it's up to you if you want to talk about it or not."

Ella blushes and looks down at the table. "You and Tucker have that same knack of disarming me. And, as usual, you're right. I do have something on my mind."

Raising her head, she looks at him directly. "I want to tell you how much I enjoy your company. I enjoy talking with you. You're a good listener. That's something Jack never was. And you don't look at me like I'm damaged or ugly just because I've had cancer and surgery. You make me feel like a whole person. Next to my father, you're the most honest, sincere, caring man I've ever known." She slides her hand across the table toward him. "I feel safe with you."

Carter covers her thin hand with his. He resists the urge to speak. He senses this is very important to Ella and that there is more to come.

She blushes again and averts her eyes. "I enjoy being around your masculinity. It makes me feel alive, alive in a way that's been dead for a long time." She pauses and takes a deep breath. Letting it out slowly, she looks back at his face. "That's why I want to ask you to do something for me."

Carter's head is spinning as he searches every corner of his imagination to try and guess what she could say next. Suddenly his eyes grow wide as he realizes what she is going to ask. "Ella," he begins, but she shushes him.

"Let me get this out while I've still got my nerve," she says. "Irvin, I want to lie in bed with you. I want you to hold me. Nothing more. Just hold me."

Fear touches the edges of her eyes as questions crowd her mind. *Will he think I'm foolish? Will he be repulsed by my request?*

Carter gently squeezes her hand. "Let me tell you something first. My wife has been the only woman I've ever loved. When God took her from me when she gave birth to our son, I closed off that part of my heart. I put everything I had into raising our son. And, then, when God took him, too, well . . . my life became dark. I didn't care about nothing. I was mean. I used women. I drank a lot. My life was hollow. And now you reach out to me. You have touched my heart and warmed it. The only thing I ask of you is don't ever leave me alone."

He rises from his chair and pulls her up to him. Leading her, he takes her to his bedroom.

As they stand beside the bed, he says huskily, "You just tell me what to do."

"Let's just lie down on top of the covers," Ella says nervously. "I'll lie on my side and you lie behind me on your side."

Without waiting for a response, she slips off her shoes, crawls onto the bed, and lies on her side. She hears Carter unlacing his boots and dropping them heavily to the floor.

The springs in the bed groan as he lifts himself onto the opposite side from her. She waits breathlessly, her eyes wide. Then she feels the mattress begin to sag as he shifts his weight toward her.

Moving as carefully as he would if he were handling nitroglycerin, Carter lets his body barely touch Ella's.

Ella's eyes close and tears begin to fall. She gently pushes herself into him.

Feeling her response, Carter rests completely against her and puts his arm over her.

When Carter's body heat weaves its way through her clothes and touches her skin, Ella sobs softly.

Carter lets her cry.

She puts her arms around his arm and pulls it tightly to her.

They lie like this for quite some time. Ella's crying subsides and her breathing evens out.

Carter's breathing becomes slow and rhythmic.

"Irvin," she whispers.

"Mmmm?" he answers sleepily.

"I'm scared."

No response.

"Irvin? I think my cancer is back."

Carter's soft snoring is the only answer she receives.

CHAPTER EIGHTEEN

Sitting on the edge of her hospital bed, Ella shivers as she tries to close the gaps in her hospital gown. *Why are hospitals always so cold? It's ridiculous!*

She looks down at her feet and notices that her toenails have a purplish hue. She clenches and unclenches her feet, trying to increase the circulation.

This is her second day at the Baptist Hospital in downtown Memphis. Yesterday was filled with tests—X-rays, blood work—and interviews by numerous student interns from the University of Tennessee School of Medicine. It's a blur to her, as if she is in a daze. With every test and every fresh-faced intern there was an eerie sense of déjà vu from her battle with breast cancer years ago.

Today she reported to the familiar oncology floor. The smells were the same and it seemed that the patients tethered to IV poles and walking haltingly in the hallways were the same, too. They were all in different stages of losing their hair, from patchy bald spots to total absence of hair—eyebrows and eyelashes included.

Their hollow expressions touched a place in her as deep and dark as Mammoth Cave. Ella refused to lock eyes with any of the patients. Words like *fear, hopelessness,* and *sadness* echoed in the chambers of her heart like pebbles dropped into a well.

There is a sharp rap on her door.

Ella's head jerks up. Her heart hammers like the hoofbeats of a speeding horse. "Come in," she says.

The door swings wide and a heavyset man strides in followed by an entourage of wide-eyed interns. They are dressed in white lab coats and every doctor's first tool, the stethoscope, hangs around their necks.

Stopping a few feet from Ella's bed, their leader reaches to the top of his bald head and retrieves a pair of glasses. Putting them on, he scans the chart that is handed to him. He barely begins reading when he stops and looks up at Ella. His demeanor softens.

"Ella McDade," he says warmly and extends his hand.

"Hello again, Charlie," Ella says as she reaches for his hand.

The young gaggle of interns exchange confused looks.

Noticing this, Ella smiles and says, "I mean, Dr. Majors."

The doctor waves his hand dismissively at his students. "Don't pay any attention to those minions. My goodness, how long has it been? And how is Jack?"

"Jack divorced me soon after my mastectomy."

Charlie's face darkens. "That coldhearted bastard. I never liked him, even when you two were dating at Ole Miss. Remember?"

"Yes, I do." Ella nods. "I was looking for the wrong things back then. I should have accepted your invitation to the campus play that first weekend we were freshmen." She smiles wanly. "I chose the wrong beau."

He gently releases her hand. As he does, he slips into his air of professionalism as if he were donning a familiar sport coat. He is a teacher again. Turning to the student on his right, he says, "Give us the case history, Scott."

The nervous student dutifully reads the record of Ella's family health history.

As the student nears the end of the record, Dr. Majors cuts him off and says, "Connie, what is the more recent history with this patient?"

A young woman stands confidently and, without referring to any notes, uses a detached tone to recite a clean, polysyllabic version of Ella's battle with breast cancer, including the surgery and chemotherapy.

"Which brings us to the present," Dr. Majors says. "Who has the current test results? Hand me the file."

An intern at the back of the circle extends an arm, a metal file in his hand. Dr. Majors takes it and opens it. He quietly flips through some pages.

Closing the chart, he returns his glasses to their perch atop his dome. Looking Ella in the eye, he says, "And so the wolf has returned. As I'm sure you guessed, you have lung cancer." He pauses, giving her an opening to speak if she desires to.

"No, I'm not surprised," Ella says. "All I need to know is how bad it is."

"What's important," Charlie says, "is that we get started immediately with chemotherapy so we can return the beast to his cave. We have made lots of advances since you were here before."

"It's that bad, huh?" Ella asks.

Charlie shoves his hands into the pockets of his lab coat. "Yes, Ella, it's bad. Stage four. It can happen this way sometimes. That is, there will be no symptoms of any problems at all until suddenly the patient gets a cough, goes to the doctor, and there it is—the rabid wolf is back."

"How much time do I have?" Ella asks.

"Well, I don't think we need to waste any time. We need to start tomorrow."

"That's not what I'm asking. I'm asking you to tell me how much longer I have to live."

The troop of interns shift nervously and look preoccupied with a notebook, a broken fingernail, a pen that suddenly won't write, a button that doesn't seem to want to fasten. Connie, the young intern who spoke earlier, takes a half step closer to Ella. "Mrs. McDade, we believe you can have many more years of life. You defeated cancer once before. You know it can be beaten again."

Ella gives her a kind smile. "It's Connie, isn't it?"

"Yes, ma'am."

"Can I ask you a question, Connie?"

Charlie steps a bit to the side, allowing his old friend and the young intern to face each other.

"Of course you can," Connie replies confidently.

The rest of the interns are now riveted on watching one of their peers have the opportunity to talk with a patient one-on-one.

"How long do you intend to live, Connie?" Ella asks.

Though delivered lightly, the blow from the unexpected question knocks Connie off of her tightwire of confidence. She hesitates. "I'm . . . I'm not sure what you mean."

Ella's eyes widen. "Really? It's a pretty straightforward question. How long do you intend to live?"

Connie glances at Dr. Majors. His expression tells her she is alone on this ice floe. She will have to resort to her own wits.

"I don't think I've ever sat down and put a number on it," Connie replies carefully. She senses that this patient is plumbing depths that she has never explored. "I think eighty or eighty-five would be a full life."

"And that's where you would be wrong," Ella says calmly. "Are you living now, Connie?"

For the first time, Connie breaks eye contact and shifts uncomfortably on her feet.

"I'm sorry," Ella says. "I don't mean to put you on the spot." She glances at each of the interns. Their eyes are riveted on her. "Connie said that eighty or eighty-five would be a full life. A full life. But the number of years a person lives has nothing to do with whether or not they've lived a full life. Eighty years is a lot of years, I guess, when compared to twenty years. But just because a person has lived a lot of years doesn't mean they've lived a full life."

Ella breaks off her intense focus on Connie and turns to Charlie. "My question is, how long do I have to live if I do nothing about this cancer?"

The doctor side of Charlie Majors considers protesting what Ella is implying. But the resolute set of her jaw tells him he would be wasting his time. In a gentle tone he says, "Three months at the least. Nine months at the most."

"That'll be just enough time," Ella says. "If you'll get my discharge papers in order, I need to be heading home."

Dr. Majors snaps his fingers toward the somber-looking group of students. An intern at the back spins on his heels and heads out the door to do his bidding.

Charlie takes Ella's hand between his hands and says, "I don't have to agree with you. But I do respect your right to do things your own way. I'll be in touch."

"Thank you, Charlie."

An hour later Ella is sitting in the chair of her hospital room, overnight bag on the floor beside her, waiting for the required wheelchair ride from this place of healing and death. There is a small tap on her door.

"It's about time," she mutters under her breath. "Come in," she calls out.

The door swings open. The shiny metal of a wheelchair appears. Connie is pushing it.

Surprised, Ella says, "Hi, Connie. I didn't expect an intern to be my chauffeur."

"I asked if I could," Connie replies. As she approaches Ella with the chariot, she says, "Mrs. McDade, can I ask you something before I take you to the elevator?"

Ella lets go of the overnight bag that she has just reached down to pick up. "Of course you can."

Connie relinquishes her hold on the wheelchair and leans back against the bed. "You asked me if I was living now. What did you mean by that?"

Ella waves dismissively. In a casual tone, she says, "Oh, that was just the ramblings of an old woman. Don't pay any attention to me."

"I don't think so," Connie says seriously. "That is, I don't think that it was just the ramblings of an old woman. I think there was meaning behind it. This will probably sound weird, but it's like you know something I don't know. That's the way I felt when you said it."

Ella drops her nonchalant demeanor. "Then let me tell you what I've learned," she says intently. "It wasn't until these last five years of my life that I've lived a full life. The years before were spent in shallowness, like I was sleepwalking through life. But five years ago I met a woman, a most unusual woman, who grabs every moment by the throat and shakes out of it everything she can. She takes life on its terms, but she definitely does it her way. She's comfortable in her own skin and makes no apologies for who she is.

"So now," Ella continues, "I try hard to live one day at a time and live each day to its fullest. I'm not waiting until I reach a certain position or juncture in my life to start enjoying life. I enjoy today, no matter what today brings."

As Ella speaks, Connie's eyes redden. She moves to Ella's chair and squats beside her. Gripping the arm of the chair, she says, "Then why, if you have learned this important lesson, don't you want to do everything you can to live as long as you can? How can you just let the cancer take your life from you?"

Ella gently pats Connie's cheek and, using her thumb, wipes off the tear that has wormed its way past Connie's professional training.

"Connie, cancer can only kill me. It can't take life from me. I have stared death in the face before and trembled in fear. But not anymore. I now know how to live even though death is lurking close by."

Connie closes her eyes and shakes her head. Opening her eyes, she says, "I'm trying to understand, but it just doesn't make sense."

"I know," Ella says. "I suppose if anyone had told me what I've told you when I was your age, I wouldn't have understood either. But just remember what I've said and tuck it away somewhere. It might make more sense and be helpful in the future."

"I will," Connie replies. Taking hold of the wheelchair, she says, "Are you ready for your free ride?"

Ella grabs her overnight bag and transfers to the wheelchair. "Onward, driver."

CHAPTER NINETEEN

With a butcher knife in her right hand, Tucker bends over and grabs a large handful of the dark green leaves in her left. She slices easily through the base of the vegetation and pitches the leaves into a bushel basket, where they join a thick pile of their former neighbors.

A flash in her peripheral vision catches Tucker's attention. Her head turns and she sees the bright sun reflecting off the windshield of Ella's approaching car. A slight smile appears.

She watches as Ella stops in front of the barn, gets out of her car, and walks toward the garden patch where Tucker is standing.

Tucker bows and waves her arm like a maître d'. "Welcome t' m' world. How'dja like a mess o' turnip greens?"

Ella fastens the top button of her coat and pulls her scarf more tightly to her scalp. "How can you stand this cold wind without a jacket on? I think this is our coldest morning yet."

"It's gotta be a lot colder than this fer me t' put on a coat. It feels good to me." Pointing to the brimming basket of leafy greens, she says, "Y' need some of 'em. It'll put iron in yore blood an' pink in yore cheeks. I noticed y' been lookin' sorta pale lately."

Ella shivers in spite of herself. "Yes, I'll take some back with me. Since you taught me how to prepare them, I've really learned to like them. I think I've got an empty grocery sack in my car."

Tucker notices Ella's lips taking on a purplish hue and her quivering chin. "Lord, woman! You're freezin' t' death. I'll grab a handful o' greens an' walk with y' t' yore car. Then you can put 'em in that sack. No sense in y' havin' to walk back an' forth t' th' car."

Tucker leans over and thrusts her beefy hand into the basket. When she pulls it out, the loose turnip leaves look like they're trying to escape through her fingers. They flap in the wind, looking like they will take flight and return to the basket. But nothing ever escapes from Tucker's grip. Nothing.

When they get to the car, Ella opens the back door, reaches in, and brings out a large paper grocery sack. She holds it open with two hands as Tucker stuffs it full of the iron-rich vegetable. Smiling, Ella says, "Those will be really good."

She opens the front door and starts to get in when she stops. "Silly me, I almost forgot why I came here in the first place. You know Thanksgiving is next Thursday."

Nodding, Tucker says, "Yeah, I think one o' 'em kids tol' me it was. They's all excited 'bout havin' a break from school."

"April certainly is," Ella agrees. "You know, for the past few years you and the children have joined me at the house for the Thanksgiving meal."

Tucker senses change is coming. And she is tired of change.

"I was thinking," Ella says slowly. "I was thinking about asking Smiley Carter and Shady Green to eat with us. Everyone could bring their instruments and we could have a music session after the meal. What do you think?"

Tucker folds her arms across her chest. "I ain't got nothin' 'gainst either one o' 'em. If'n y' wanta ask 'em, it'll be okay by me." Noticing Ella's pensive expression, Tucker drops her arms to her side. Making an effort to smile, she says, "Besides, it might be a lotta fun."

Ella's face softens and she smiles. "I was hoping you would agree. It's just important to me to have all the people that matter to me gathered together for a day of thanksgiving. Now, you'll cook one of your famous hams, won't you?"

Tucker stands straighter and sticks out her ample, though sagging, chest. "Best hams in th' state. That's what I say. Sure thing, I'll fix one. An' I'll dig some sweet taters an' cook some o' them, too. Will that be good?"

Ella pats the top of Tucker's chest. "Good for you! That will be delicious!"

CHAPTER TWENTY

Thanksgiving morning Tucker comes bustling through the back door carrying an armload of firewood. August follows right on her heels carrying an equally heavy load of wood.

As they pass through the kitchen, the rich smell of ham drifts from the oven. Arriving in the living room, Tucker drops her load into the box beside the woodstove. "Y' done a real good job o' splittin' this here wood, August. There's a piece 'r two o' elm in here an' it can be th' devil t' split."

August drops his cargo on top of hers. Small pieces of bark and a few long, thin splinters bounce off the wood and land on the floor around the box. Gingerly opening the door of the hot stove, he thrusts two sticks of wood into the waiting bed of hungry coals. Trying to appear nonchalant, he says, "It wasn't nothing to it. With me using the splitting maul and sledgehammer, that wood didn't stand a chance."

Tucker rests her hand on his shoulder. Looking him in the eye, she says, "Y' really been growin' up, August. Y' becomin' a fine young man. I'm proud o' y'."

Feeling uncomfortable with this unusual praise from Tucker, August says, "You need any help in the kitchen?"

"No, I'm good. If y' go feed th' animals, I'll git busy with m' taters."

In Ella's house, April is folding napkins and giving the edge a crease with the side of her hand, just the way Ella showed her. The new full-size dining table that was delivered yesterday looks twice as long as the small breakfast table it replaced. "I've never seen this many plates and glasses in my life," she exclaims. "And they all match!"

Ella looks up from the bowl of meringue she is mixing. As she turns on the mixer, she says, "And you did a beautiful job of putting everything perfectly into place. I decided I just had to have a table big enough for everyone to sit around. Aren't you excited about having everyone over?"

April joins her grandmother to watch the meringue begin its transformation into white puffy clouds of sweetness. "Yes, it's going to be fun. But I can't help thinking about March. I wonder if he's having a Thanksgiving meal somewhere."

Ella aches because of the longing she hears in April's voice. "Yes, I do, too, April. But always remember this: don't ever let your focus be so much on the one cloud in the sky that you miss noticing the unending expanse of beautiful blue and the brilliant, shining sun all around. What I do know for sure is that wherever March is, he would want us to enjoy ourselves. Don't you agree?"

April cautiously slips one finger to the edge of the bowl and swipes a dollop of meringue. After she sucks it off, she says, "Yes, ma'am, you're right."

Ella turns off the beaters and, using a plastic spatula, piles the meringue on top of the waiting sea of chocolate in the pie dish. Then she slides it into the warm oven.

Just then they hear the sound of an engine out front.

"It sounds like Smiley Carter," April says, as she goes dashing toward the front door.

"Let them in," Ella calls to her.

As April opens the door, she sees Smiley Carter alighting from his tractor seat and Shady Green jumping off one of the rear fenders. "Ya'll come on in," she says from the front porch.

At the sound of her voice, Carter looks up. His face breaks into a celebration—eyes dancing, dimples winking, and his famous smile. "You are as pretty as the morning sun shining on the dew! Come here and give ol' Smiley a hug!"

April dashes off the porch and leaps into his waiting arms. She hugs his neck. His normally prickly face is smooth and she detects the smell of Old Spice.

"Goodness, girl," Carter says, "I used to throw you into the air like you was a ball. But not no more. You're becoming a big girl." He sets her down.

April brushes the wrinkles out of her new dress and says matter-of-factly, "I am a big girl."

Shady Green comes from around the side of the tractor. "Ehwoh, A'ril."

"Hi, Shady," she replies. "Ya'll follow me in."

"Let's get my banjo and your guitar off the hood of the tractor and take them in out of the cold," Carter says to Shady.

"Eh-sir," Shady answers and unfastens the makeshift leather straps.

With their instruments in hand, Carter says to April, "Lead the way, madam."

Walking through the front door produces an olfactory assault on the two men. They both inhale deeply. Carter closes his eyes and says, "I smell fresh rolls, a baked turkey, cinnamon, chocolate, coffee, corn . . ."

Shady chimes in, "An' gwee bea's."

"Yes, sir," Carter says with a laugh, "and green beans."

They set the guitar and banjo down and begin unfastening their heavy coats. When Carter slips off his denim jumper he reveals a powder-blue dress shirt with a button-down collar.

April whistles.

Just then Ella walks into the living room wiping her hands on a hand towel.

"Doesn't he look nice?" April says admiringly.

Ella's taken aback by Carter's polished appearance and stands staring.

Breaking the awkward silence, Carter strikes a pose and says, "You all will probably see me on the cover of the next issue of *GQ* magazine."

Everyone laughs.

Ella walks forward to greet her visitors. "I'm so glad you two came." Noticing the banjo and guitar cases, she adds, "And that you brought your instruments. Just have a seat and make yourselves at home. I'm still busy in the kitchen."

Just as the men start to sit down, there is the sound of heavy footsteps on the porch, then two heavy blows at the base of the front door.

"Tucker!" April squeals. She darts to the door and flings it open.

Tucker's bulk fills the doorway. In each hand there is a large picnic basket. She turns sideways so she can squeeze through the opening. Spying Carter and Shady Green, she says, "Jes' like a couple o' men t' stand 'round watchin' a woman what needs helpin'."

The two men spring into action like a couple of schoolboys.

"Here, let us help you," Carter says, reaching for a basket.

Tucker swivels to block the attempt. "I ain't got but ten more feet t' go. Ya'll jes' do what y' do best an' stay out o' th' way."

August then steps through the open door carrying two five-gallon buckets.

Carter beams as he looks at the boy. "Shady, ain't that the finest-looking young man you ever seen?"

"'Im shoo isss," Shady agrees.

"What's in the buckets?" Carter asks as August passes by.

Shrugging his shoulders, August says, "Pots of food stacked up on pots of food. That's all I know."

"What about Tucker's ham?" Carter whispers loudly. "Did she cook a ham?"

August smiles and winks. "No problem," he whispers back.

After a few minutes, the call they are all eager for comes from the kitchen. "Let's all have a seat," Ella says.

As they start finding a place to sit, Ella says, "Wait just a minute."

Everyone stops and looks toward their host.

"Smiley, I want you to sit here at the head of the table. I'll sit on your right so I can get to the kitchen easily. April, you sit beside me. Then, Tucker, you sit at the other end of the table. August, you sit to Smiley's left. And, Shady, you sit beside August."

Everyone shifts around the table according to Ella's instructions.

Once everyone is seated, they pause expectantly.

"I'd like to ask Smiley to offer thanks for our blessings," Ella says. "And I'd like for us all to hold hands."

Hands are clasped around the table and heads bow.

Carter's rich baritone voice fills the air. "Our Lord God in heaven above. It is with hearts full of thankfulness that we praise you. No one has ever seen the limits of your love and mercy. For this bountiful feast, one that many folks will never have, we praise you. For bringing all of us into each other's lives, we praise you. Of the twists and turns of life, only you, God, see the path. But we trust that wherever March is this day, he will know we all love him and, especially, that you love him. In the name of our blessed savior we pray, amen."

There is a collective sound of sniffing noses as Carter's prayer ends. "Let the feast begin," he says.

CHAPTER TWENTY-ONE

Scooting his chair back from the table and laying his folded napkin on his plate, Carter says, "I believe that was the finest Thanksgiving meal I ever ate."

"Mmmm-mmmm," is all the comment Shady Green can muster.

"Before everyone starts falling asleep in their chairs," Ella says, "let's play some music. Bring some of the chairs into the living room. I'll go get my Autoharp."

Moving rather sluggishly, everyone follows Ella's directions.

Once everyone is in a circle, Carter says, "Give us a G, Ella. We'll tune to you."

Ella strums a G chord, and Carter and Shady Green bend their heads low to their instruments, plucking strings and twisting tuning keys. Once satisfied, Carter gives a loud strum on his banjo. Shady Green smiles and responds in similar fashion. Ella completes the process by echoing the same chord.

"Just right," Carter says.

"Kick off 'Foggy Mountain Breakdown,'" Ella says. "Let's chase away the sandman and put some life into this room."

Halfway through the first verse, April lifts her dress to her knees and begins clogging. Tucker and August clap in rhythm.

For the next forty minutes the songs come fast and furious, as someone calls out the name of another song as soon as one ends. Finally, Carter pulls out his bandanna and, wiping his sweating face, says, "I believe I've done sweated out all the grease I ate at lunch. I'm about to render lard!"

Everyone laughs at his hyperbole.

"Before we quit," Ella says, "I'd like to do an old song that's close to my heart called 'White.'" Nodding at Carter and Shady Green, she says, "You boys just follow me."

She begins a light strumming on her Autoharp and sings:

Ye fleeting charms of earth farewell,
Your springs of joy are dry;
My soul seeks another home.
A brighter world on high.
I'm a long time trav'ling here below,
I'm a long time trav'ling away from home,
I'm a long time trav'ling here below,
To lay this body down.
Farewell, my friends, whose tender care
Has long engaged my love;
Your fond embrace I now exchange
For better friends above.
I'm a long time trav'ling here below,
To lay this body down.

Halfway through the song, April sits at Ella's feet and rests her head against her legs, feeling the vibrations of the Autoharp.

When the song is over, no one says a word. They are struck by the special meaning they find in its lyrics. Tucker turns her head and blows her nose.

As Ella looks up from her Autoharp, they can see the shining tears on her cheeks. Her voice choked with emotion, she says, "I want all of you to know that these past few years that I've called this place home have been nothing short of heaven. Each one of you . . ." She pauses to look from face to face. ". . . has brought something special to my life. These last years have been the best years of my life."

Tucker clears her throat and scoots forward in her seat. Looking at the floor she opens her mouth to speak, but nothing comes out. She clears her throat again. "An' y', Ella, y' brung somethin' out here when y' come. I study 'bout it from time t' time, tryin' t' fig'r out what it is. One o' these days I will. But I'll tell y', it's somethin' I ain't never had b'fore."

Ella smiles appreciatively at her friend. "Well, while I've still got a few ounces of energy left, we better start cleaning up those dishes."

CHAPTER TWENTY-TWO

Smiley Carter pulls up the collar of his heavy denim jumper to cover his ears and fastens the top button to hold it tightly in place. Pulling his fleece-lined leather work gloves from the pocket, he slips his hands inside.

Stepping outside the back door of his house, the sharp December wind slaps him in the face, taking his breath. There is an occasional stinging of sleet in the cold front that has swept into the area.

He walks to his tractor and, while standing beside it, engages the ignition. The cold engine turns over reluctantly. Carter pulls out the choke to encourage his dependable vehicle to start. "Come on, Bessie," he coaxes.

Like a horse responding to the familiar sound of its owner, the tractor jumps to life. Carter eases the choke in and lets the engine idle long enough to get all the fluids running freely.

Carter replays the brief phone call that has gotten him out on such a raw day, a phone call that has left his heart full of apprehension.

"Irvin, this is Ella."

"Hi, Ella," he replies. "How are you?"

DAVID JOHNSON

"Irvin, I know this is a horrible day to be outside, but can you come over for a little bit?"

There is something in her tone of voice that causes a quiet alarm to go off in Carter's brain. "Is there anything wrong?" he asks.

"I've just got something I want to talk to you about," Ella replies, trying to keep her voice even. "Plus, I've just taken an apple pie out of the oven. You know you don't want to miss that."

"Well, sure, Ella," Carter replies. "If you want me to come over, I'll be right there. Tell that pie to enjoy its final few moments because I'm coming to put it out of its misery." He laughs.

Carter now realizes what it was in the conversation that triggered his worry. At the end of the call, Ella didn't respond to his laughter with her own laughter, something she never failed to do.

He searches for meaning. If she wanted to talk about good news, she would have easily told him outright over the phone. So it can't be anything pleasant. But what?

He climbs onto his tractor, puts it into gear, and lets out on the clutch. As if his action engaged his heart, too, a tear forms at the corner of his eye. He swipes it with the back of his glove.

"Silly old man," he says aloud as he pulls out of the shed. "You're worrying about something when it might be nothing."

Thirty minutes later he pulls up in front of Ella's house. The bitter wind on the ride over has triggered more tears and streaked them from Carter's eyes back to his temples. His nose has produced a thin flow that runs over his upper lip, but his face is so numb he is oblivious to what is happening. Only when he tastes the salty fluid does he realize it. Taking out his blue bandanna, he wipes his mouth and blows his nose.

As he walks stiffly to the porch, Ella opens the front door. He is immediately struck by her pale complexion. As if his earlier alarms have only been briefly silenced by a snooze button, they suddenly

106

release a cacophony of dissonant sounds. Carter feels an old feeling of pain in his chest.

"Hurry in here before you freeze," Ella says.

"Old men don't hurry," Carter says smiling. Walking into the house, he adds, "Did I ever tell you the story about the young bull and the old bull?"

Knowing she's probably in for a story with a tease in it, Ella smiles and says, "I don't believe you have. But I'm sure you're about to fill me in."

Carter begins taking off his gloves and coat. "Well, you see there was this old, wise bull. He was quite content with his life on the farm. One day the farmer brings a young bull and turns him out in the pasture with the old bull."

"I notice," Ella says with a twinkle in her eye, "that the old bull is the wise one."

Carter holds up his hand. "Don't get ahead of the story now."

He follows her into the kitchen and takes his familiar place at the table where a piece of pie is sitting. He puts a bite in his mouth and savors the warm sweetness.

Ella sits across from him.

"Okay, now where was I?" he says. "Oh, yes. This young bull shows up. He asks the old bull what he does for fun, where the sweetest grass is, where the cleanest water is—those kinds of questions.

"Suddenly the young bull looks up at the top of a knoll in the pasture where there are twelve to fifteen cattle. 'What's that up there?' he asks the old bull.

"'Oh,' says the old bull nonchalantly, 'them is the herd of new heifers turned out this morning. We are responsible for breeding them.'

'Young heifers?' the young bull says, his tongue hanging out. With a lustful look he says, 'Let's run to the top of the hill and take care of some of them.'"

Carter pauses for effect and takes another bite of pie. Looking at Ella with a smile, he says, "That's when the old bull says, 'Let's just walk to the top of the hill and we can take care of *all* of them.'"

It takes Ella a second to get the gist of the story. She blushes and laughs. "Now I know why you called the old bull wise. And that's why you don't get in a hurry?"

Carter laughs. "Yessiree, this is one fine piece of pie."

Their laughter dies down and is replaced by heaviness in the air. Carter feels a chill on the back of his neck. He fixes his eyes on Ella.

"Irvin," she says, "thank you so much for coming over. It's a bitter day outside but I've had something I've been needing to talk to you about. I decided today I had to get it done."

Carter searches Ella's face to see if he can find any indication of what is about to come next. It is the unknown that has him spooked.

"Whatever it is," he says, "let's get it out in the open so we can look at it together. When you look at something all by yourself it can sometimes become bigger than it has to be. Maybe it's time for you to share whatever you've been keeping to yourself."

Ella takes a deep breath and lets it out slowly. She fixes her eyes on the table. "There is no easy way to say this. And you're the first person I've shared it with." She lifts her eyes to look at his. Sliding her hands across the table, she says, "Hold my hands."

Carter carefully wraps his large, warm, dark hands around her frail, cold, pale hands.

"Irvin, I have cancer."

CHAPTER TWENTY-THREE

Of all the hypothetical ideas Carter had about why Ella had brought him out on such a day, he had never even considered cancer. He feels as if he has walked into his house and been struck on the back of the neck with a baseball bat wielded by an intruder hiding behind the door. His breath leaves him.

He hears himself say the word *cancer* aloud in a hoarse whisper. But he can't engage his brain to work, to make any kind of sense of what Ella has said. There are only snippets of thoughts fluttering through his mind like pieces of confetti, but nothing that is logical.

A thought coalesces as he sees Ella's face and her expression of concern. "But I thought you was cured of your cancer," he says, still searching for meaning.

Her shoulders slump. "Yes, I know. I was cured of breast cancer. But unfortunately I've learned that I now have lung cancer. I went to Memphis last month and saw my cancer doctor. There is no doubt about the diagnosis."

Carter squeezes her hands. "But cancer ain't nothing for you. You've whipped it before and you can whip it again. I'll be right here to help you. And Tucker will, too."

Ella shakes her head slowly. She pulls her hands from inside his grasp and places them on top of his hands. "Not this time, Irvin. Not this time."

Carter shakes his head, trying to clear it of yet another piece of information that doesn't fit. "What are you talking about? What do you mean, 'not this time'?"

Ella gets up. She takes a chair from the side of the table and slides it up against Carter's chair. She sits down and slips her arm under his and places both hands on his forearm. "Irvin, the doctor says I only have three to nine months to live."

Carter feels his heart stop. He turns to look into her face, searching for any sign that she is playing some kind of sadistic trick on him. He notices that her high cheekbones look more pronounced than usual. Her cheeks are a bit sunken. He begins shaking his head. "No, no, no. It's not true. It can't be true."

Ella nods her head. "But it is true, Irvin."

He jumps up from the table. A cry comes from deep within his soul that rends the air and tears Ella's heart. Like a mighty oak toppled by a storm, he falls to his knees and looks up. Tears stream down his face. "Lord God above, my strong right hand, my rock, my shelter, make me wake up from this nightmare! Deliver me from this awful place. Tell me this is not real. Do not do this to me again! My soul will not survive it."

Ella goes to him and kneels in front of him. Her face is flushed and drenched in her own tears. "Irvin," she says earnestly. "Listen to me. I need you. If ever I needed you, it is now. I know that is selfish of me. This news is painful for you and the end will be—"

She is startled as Carter draws back his arm as if to strike her with his open palm.

His hand hurtles toward her but stops an inch from her face. Putting his hand tenderly over her mouth, he puts his face within inches of hers and in a hoarse whisper says, "Do not utter it. Do not speak the words. Do you understand me?"

Ella gives her head a quick nod.

Carter takes his hand away from her mouth and wipes her tears with his thumbs. "Anything can happen. God can work a miracle. The doctors might be wrong—" His voice breaks. With the voice of a child he says, "You promised."

Puzzled, Ella says, "Promised?"

"You promised not to leave me. Remember?"

Ella takes his face in her hands. "Listen to me, Irvin. One of the refreshing things about my life out here is the honesty. I learned it first from Tucker, then from her grandchildren, and lastly from you. If I can't be honest with you during this, then everything that has happened between us means nothing." She gives his face a gentle jerk. "I need you to be with me to the end. I cannot do this by myself. Do you understand?"

Like a child who has been chastised for an outburst, Carter submits and nods meekly.

"So, I can count on you?" Ella asks.

Carter surrounds Ella's face with his hands. His tears dry. In a clear voice, he says, "Whatever lies in your path from this day to your last, I will be there with you every step of the way. Say anything you want. Ask anything. I will be the one who will be there."

Ella smiles. "That's what I wanted to hear."

They help each other stand up. She leans against his strong chest. He envelopes her in his arms. They stand for several moments, feeling each other's heartbeat.

"Have you told Tucker?" Carter asks.

"No," Ella says softly, "nor April."

CHAPTER TWENTY-FOUR

Tucker pitches three more towels onto the heap of clothes that she has piled on top of a bedsheet lying on her floor. Grasping the four corners of the sheet, she pulls them up and ties them in a knot, securing the bulging contents inside. She drags the heavy, awkward bulk to the front door much the same way she used to drag a cotton sack when she handpicked cotton as a child.

Opening the door, she steps through and drags her burden onto the porch. She looks up to see Ella driving into her front yard. When Ella steps out of her car, Tucker says, "It's Tuesday warsh day, ain't it?"

"Yes, indeed," Ella answers as she approaches the porch. "And it appears you've got a pretty good load of dirty clothes there."

Tucker places her hands on her hips. "You'd think an ol' woman who practic'ly lives by 'erself wouldn't have hardly any dirty clothes. But somehow I manage t' have a purty good load ever' week."

As Ella reaches Tucker's side, she bends over and grabs part of Tucker's bundle. "Here, let me help you get this to the car."

Tucker resists her usual urge to protest against Ella's help. "That'd be nice," she says.

Carrying the awkward bundle between them, the two women walk sideways toward the car. They heave it into the open trunk and slam the lid shut.

Ella leans against the closed trunk and gasps for breath.

When they get inside the car, Ella comments, "Isn't it an unusually warm day for December? It was colder than this in November."

"You're right. Winter 'round here can be awful unpredictable. I've seen th' time when we had a killin' frost b'fore Thanksgiving, then it'll warm up in December t' where it feels like spring. That's what makes ever'body git sick."

"I'd forgotten that," Ella says. "It's been an especially unusual weather year this year. Remember when we had that late frost this spring?"

"Don't I fer sure! It was late April. Th' dogwoods was in full bloom and I done had some early corn comin' up in m' garden. It was what we used t' call an unexpected frost. Killed my corn and turned all th' dogwood blooms brown."

"You're right. I remember how sad all those dogwood trees looked. Like it killed their souls to have to let go of their beautiful flowers, almost like they felt they'd let them down by not protecting them."

"Sure enough," Tucker replies. "It was jes' when ever'thing was bustin' out an' lookin' purty. That's why them unexpected frosts is th' worse kind."

Once they arrive at Ella's house, they manage to wrestle Tucker's load of dirty laundry onto the back porch. The washer and dryer wait silently, like children who mean to be seen but not heard and thereby might avoid the heavy workload that Tuesday always brings.

Ella releases her grip on the corner of the bundle of dirty laundry and coughs. She winces and grabs her side, turning to hide her pain from Tucker.

"I always hated warsh day b'fore we started doin' it t'gether," Tucker says. "Now I don't mind it at all."

Smiling, Ella says, "I like it, too. It's a good time to visit. And it doesn't seem like it takes near as long to get it done."

Tucker pats the dryer firmly. "Never thought I'd like havin' clothes that wasn't dried on a clothesline. But this here contraption sure makes clothes extry soft."

Ella laughs. "And I used to think you were crazy for hanging clothes out in freezing temperatures. The shirts and pants used to look like they were double starched they were frozen so stiff."

Tucker unties her bundle of clothes and begins sorting them. "We doin' th' dark things first?"

"I think that works best," Ella replies. "They take the longest to dry."

Later in the morning Ella takes a load out of the dryer and carries it to the dining table. The two women stand on either side of the table and begin folding the warm clothes.

Tucker holds up one of April's dresses. "Now ain't that th' purtiest little dress y' ever seen? I bet she looks like an angel in this."

Ella smiles. "Yes, she does. As a matter of fact, April looks good in nearly everything she wears."

Tucker picks up another piece of clothing and notices Ella staring at her. "What?" Tucker asks.

Embarrassed at having been caught staring, Ella blurts, "Nothing. Nothing. Just thinking."

Tucker stops what she's doing. "Oh good Lord, woman. Spit it out. As much as y' an' me been through since we met, I think y' could say mighty near anythin'."

Ella averts her eyes. She picks up a shirt and begins folding it. "It's something we've never talked about, but it's something I've always been curious about."

Tucker busies herself matching socks. When Ella doesn't say anything more, Tucker says, "I'm waitin' on y'."

"Well," Ella begins, "I've always wondered why you never wear women's clothes."

In the blink of an eye Tucker finds herself lying on a bed in Mama Mattie's house, her newly born baby, Maisy, lying beside her. She hears herself telling Mama Mattie to burn all her clothes.

And, in another blink, Tucker is staring at the pile of clean clothes on Ella's table.

"Tucker?" Ella says.

Tucker shakes her head. "Huh? What?"

"Are you okay?"

Clearing her throat, Tucker says, "Course I am. Y' jes' caught me by surprise a bit. Guess that's somethin' I never—"

"Forget it," Ella says. "I'm such a nosy person sometimes. I don't know when to leave well enough alone. It's not even important. I apologize."

Very slowly, Tucker drags a chair from under the dining table and sits down. Motioning at Ella, she says, "Sit down an' I'll tell y'. Maybe it's somethin' I should o' tol' b'fore now."

Ella frowns. "Look, Tucker, you don't have to do this. Really, it's none of my business. Let's just get back to our clothes."

Tucker waves her down into a chair. "I wanta tell it."

CHAPTER TWENTY-FIVE

Ella obeys Tucker's directions and sits. "*Why, oh, why,*" she thinks to herself, "*do I have to pry? Why can't I just leave well enough alone?*"

Tucker doesn't look at Ella. She looks off into the distance. Her gaze travels across the dimensions of time and place. It is several moments before she speaks. Her voice has a thin, childlike quality.

"From as early in m' life as I have memory, m' daddy had 'is way with me. An' I don't mean he was jes' touchin' me. I mean sex.

"When I was little I would scream when it hurt. Then, when I got older, I didn't feel nothin' when he did it. I jes' lay there 'til he got through. It was sorta like I wadn't even there.

"But toward th' end I started havin' this deep, hot feelin' o' rage. An' th' older I got, th' hotter an' deeper it got. 'Til one day I decided I would end it."

Ella notices Tucker's hands slowly clenching into fists and her voice getting stronger.

"My sixteenth birthday," Tucker continues. "That's what I decided would be m' day o' freedom, m' day o' escape." She turns to look Ella in the face. "Y' hear what I'm sayin'? I wadn't gonna take it no more. I couln't take it no more. Somethin' had t' be done 'bout it an' I figured I would have t' be th' one who done it."

The intensity of Tucker's words pushes Ella back in her chair and pins her there. Ella's the one who wants to escape now because she is afraid of what she will hear next. She feels like she is in the middle of a nightmare from which she cannot wake up. She hears herself say, "Go on."

Tucker turns and her gaze returns to that far-off place and time. "The night o' m' sixteenth birthday, durin' th' middle o' a thunderstorm, he was doin' me on th' ground out near th' barn. While I was lyin' there I seen 'is hatchet on th' ground b'side me. I grabbed it and kilt him!" On these last words Tucker's fist hammers the table.

Ella screams and jumps, but Tucker seems not to notice.

"I got rid o' his body so that it wouldn't never be found. I thought I was finished with 'im an' wouldn't never have t' think 'bout 'im again." Tucker's shoulders slump and her voice sounds tired. "But I was wrong."

She looks at her friend Ella. Her eyes redden and tears begin to run down her round cheeks. "Nine months later. You hear me? Nine months later Maisy was born, with Mama Mattie at my side."

Ella feels as if her heart has turned to stone. Its weight makes it difficult for her to find her breath. She controls her facial expression so as not to reveal the horror and shock that she feels.

Tucker knows her revelation has had the force of a hammer blow on her friend, but she continues with her story. "An' that's when I decided." She looks at Ella for a reaction, as if she has ended her story.

Unsure of Tucker's meaning, Ella says, "Decided? What do you mean, 'decided'?"

"I wouldn't never be treated like that again, by nobody. I tol' Mama Mattie t' burn all m' clothes. 'Cause wearing women's clothes meant bein' a female, an' bein' a female meant bein' raped an' abused.

I ain't never wore a stitch o' women's clothes since then. An' no man has ever so much as looked like he was gonna lay his hand on me."

"Oh, Tucker . . ." Ella says in a low voice. "I wish I had been your friend back then."

"Hmph," Tucker snorts. "I don't know why. Back then you wouldn't o' give me th' time o' day. I was poor white trash. You'd o' been too good fer me."

The laser-like quality of Tucker's accusation stings Ella. She starts to protest but instead says, "You're probably right, I'm ashamed to admit."

"Course I'm right. Th' only reason you an' me had a chance t' become friends was after you had yore titties cut off, all yore hair come out, an' Judge Jack thrown y' out th' back door."

As quick as a cottonmouth striking its prey, Ella reaches across the table and slaps Tucker in the face, knocking her eyeglasses to the floor. "Damn you, you old woman! You've got no right to talk to me like that!"

Tucker stares at her, her mouth agape. Her chin begins to quiver. Color rushes to the side of her face where Ella struck her. She blinks and tears splash onto the clean clothes below her.

Ella, shocked at herself, turns pale. She slowly reaches across the table and gently touches Tucker's cheek. She tries to speak but cannot find her voice. She mouths the words, "I'm sorry."

Tucker lays her hand over Ella's and mouths back, "I'm sorry, too."

Ella turns her hand so she can grasp Tucker's hand. Squeezing it, she says, "You're the best and truest friend I've ever had."

"An' I ain't nothin' but a loudmouthed, short-tempered ol' woman who don't know when t' keep 'er mouth shut. You's the onliest person on this earth I can always depend on. I ain't sure what I'd do without y'."

Ella's eyes overflow with tears. She pulls her hand from Tucker's. Clasping her hands together on the table, she lowers her head onto them and moans, "Oh, Tucker . . ."

"Well, ain't we a sight!" Tucker exclaims. "Carryin' on like a couple o' schoolgirls with all this cryin'. We ain't never gonna git these clothes finished at this rate."

Ella looks up and opens her mouth, then closes it. Opening it again, she says, "You are right. We better get busy."

For the next several minutes they swap clothes from the washer to the dryer and fold them.

Tucker snaps the wrinkles out of a sheet. Focusing on getting the corners lined up as she folds it, she says, "Now it's m' turn t' ask y' somethin'."

Ella folds a pair of Tucker's pants and says, "Well, you certainly have the right to ask anything you want. Especially after what I ventured into a while ago."

"How come y' never fixed yoreself back up after th' cancer? I mean, I hear women can get artificial titties an' I know there's nice-lookin' wigs out there. But you never done any o' that. Y' still shave yore head even t'day. I was jes' wonderin'. . ."

Ella stops her work and looks at Tucker. Reaching up, she removes the scarf off her bald head.

"That's a fair question. It goes to what I learned from having cancer. Losing my breasts and having all my hair fall out caused me to look within to see who I truly was. I ended up having to admit that I had always been a very vain person. My looks, the outside of me, especially my breasts and hair, caused me to be prideful. It's what I often used to define myself. But when you lose what is most important to you, it gives you a chance to reevaluate things.

"So I decided I had to work on the inside of me. And if any-one was ever going to love me, they would have to love me from the inside out. That is why I have loved living out here so much.

Everyone in my world here has accepted me just as I am—scarred and bald." Smiling, she adds, "It just doesn't matter to you all."

"Lord, honey," Tucker exclaims, "that's 'cause ever'body out here has got they own scars. Yore's ain't nothin' compared t' some."

Ella looks thoughtfully at Tucker. "You know, having cancer also taught me to let go of anger and resentment. The old me would have held on forever to what Jack did to me. But after having stared death in the face, I realized that would be time wasted, and time is too precious to waste."

Like a puppy listening to a high-pitched whistle for the first time, Tucker cocks her head at Ella's words. "Y' mean y' wouldn't like to git hold o' Jack an' castrate 'im?"

Ella laughs. "Oh, I suppose I had those kinds of thoughts early on, but not in a long time."

Tucker looks dumbfounded. "How in th' world did y' let go?"

Ella looks Tucker square in the face. "Forgiveness set me free, Tucker. Forgiveness." When Tucker doesn't say anything, Ella says, "You know, you ought to think about forgiving your father."

Tucker blinks rapidly. Her mouth opens and closes repeatedly. When her voice finally engages with her thoughts, she blurts, "It'll be a cold day in hell when that happens, little lady!" Squinting, she repeats, "A cold day in hell!"

CHAPTER TWENTY-SIX

For the next thirty minutes, the women work in silence. Finally, Ella says, "I'm ready to take a break and eat some lunch. How about a fried baloney sandwich?"

Tucker looks up from her stack of folded bath towels. She smiles and says, "You, Ella McDade, fix a fried baloney sandwich?"

"Oh, hush," Ella says. "Just because I'd never heard of it before doesn't mean I didn't pay attention when you fixed me one. I had Neal at the Meat Market thick slice me some baloney right off the stick. And I've got you some Tabasco sauce, too."

Tucker slaps her thigh and laughs. "Who says y' can't teach an ol' dog new tricks or that a city gal can't learn somethin' from a country gal? Sounds delicious. I'm hungry enough t' eat th' legs off this here table."

Ella opens the drawer under her oven and grips the cast-iron skillet. As she lifts it to the stove top, the weight becomes too much and she loses her grasp. It bangs against the side of the stove and lands with a ringing thud on the floor.

Tucker cries out and jumps with a start. "What in th'—?" She sees Ella leaning against the stove, her complexion pale. As fast as her stiff knees will allow, Tucker scurries to Ella's side. "Ella, are y' all right? Did th' skillet hit yore foot? Them cast-iron skillets weigh a ton."

"I think I better sit down," Ella says weakly.

As casually as if she was picking up young April, Tucker lifts Ella off her feet and carries her to the living room. "Sit down here in yore rockin' chair an' put up yore feet on that footstool." She slides the footstool under Ella's lifted feet.

"Y' don't look good, Ella," Tucker says, frowning. "Y' got any o' my cold remedy hid in th' cabinet? It might help."

Ella holds up her hand in protest and shakes her head. "Let me catch my breath," she says in a whisper. She closes her eyes and lays her head back against the chair. Suddenly a violent cough convulses her and she bends forward. She covers her mouth with her hand as she coughs again.

Tucker looks in horror as blood oozes from between Ella's fingers. "Ella!" she screams. "Oh my God, Ella!" Adrenaline gives her the legs of her youth as she dashes into the kitchen and grabs a hand towel off the table. Rushing to Ella's side, she pulls Ella's hand away from her mouth and forces the towel to her lips.

Ella grips the towel and spits blood into it.

Tucker's wide-eyed gaze sweeps the room. Spying the telephone, she says, "Tell me how to call the amb'lance! We gotta git some help out here!"

Ella shakes her head. In a voice muffled by the towel, she says, "Help me to the bathroom." She begins to get unsteadily to her feet.

Tucker firmly grabs Ella's arm and steadies her.

When they arrive in the bathroom, Ella reaches for a cup and turns on the water. For the next few moments she swishes mouthfuls of water and spits them into the sink. Each successive one gets lighter in color until the last one is only faintly tinged with pink.

Looking into the mirror, she is shocked to see how red the blood on her face appears against her pale skin.

Tucker grabs a washcloth off the shelf and turns the warm water on. "Here, sit on th' toilet an' let me clean y' up."

Ella obeys without protest as Tucker uses the soapy cloth to remove cancer's war paint from Ella's frail face.

Content with the job she has done, Tucker says, "Now let's git y' to th' couch so y' can lie down."

After Ella settles onto the couch, Tucker covers her with an afghan. Sitting carefully on the edge of the couch, she says, "If'n y' won't let me call the amb'lance, then let me call somebody who can git us t' th' hospital."

With a touch as light as a butterfly, Ella lays her hand on Tucker's forearm. In a calm voice she says, "Go put us some water on the stove. I want a cup of hot tea."

At Ella's touch, Tucker feels an inexplicable chill. She looks over her shoulder to see if the front door has come open. Looking down at Ella, she says, "I'll see to it. Y' jes' rest until I git it fixed."

After a few minutes Tucker reenters the living room carrying two steaming mugs.

Ella sits up to receive the warm tea. She pulls her knees up toward her chest and takes a sip. Closing her eyes, she says, "Oh, yes."

Tucker sits at the end of the couch and turns so she is facing Ella. She ignores her own tea as she closely watches Ella take a few more sips. She is encouraged as some of Ella's color returns to her cheeks. "You're lookin' better. But I ain't gonna be satisfied until y' at least git seen by ol' Doc Winston."

Ella shakes her head. "No hospitals. No doctors." Seeing the puzzled expression on her friend's face, she says, "I guess now's the time."

Tucker looks perplexed. "Th' time fer what? Y' ain't makin' no sense."

Ella takes a long drink of tea then places the mug on the floor beside her. "Tucker, I've been needing to tell you something but I haven't because I've dreaded the telling. I've dreaded it because I don't want to hurt you. And this will hurt you."

Tucker opens her mouth to speak, but Ella holds up her hand. "I don't want you to say a thing until I get it all said. Okay?"

Tucker sets her still-full mug onto the floor and nods affirmatively.

"I'm going to start by saying the hardest thing first. I have cancer. Specifically, lung cancer."

Tucker grips the back of the couch.

"A few weeks ago I went to Memphis to see my cancer doctor and he confirmed the diagnosis. There is no doubt about the diagnosis and that it is very advanced."

Tucker bites down hard on her bottom lip.

"Now, here's the part that I'm afraid you are going to be upset with me about. I'm not going to get any treatments for the cancer. No radiation. No chemotherapy."

Tears fill Tucker's eyes until the bottom lid can hold no more and they cascade down her face. She begins shaking her head at Ella.

Ella feels the warmth of her own tears stinging her cheeks. "You don't understand, Tucker. You don't know what chemotherapy and radiation is like. It's like they put poison into your body with the aim of bringing you as close to death's door as they can, hoping it will kill the cancer before it kills you. It's hell. And I've been to hell and back and don't intend to return there.

"So, here's how it's going to be," she continues. "The doctor says I've only got a few months to live."

Tucker's mouth flies open and panic distorts her features. She rises slowly from the couch and stumbles toward the front door. Opening it, she goes into Ella's front yard.

Ella makes a move to go after her when suddenly she hears a cry from outside that makes her blood turn cold. It sounds as if someone has taken the scream of a screech owl and the howl of a coyote and mixed them in hell. Ella has a memory of reading *The Hound of the Baskervilles* as a child and trying to imagine what the eerie howl of the hound must have sounded like. Now she is certain she knows what it sounded like and why even the intrepid Sherlock Holmes was unnerved upon hearing it.

In a moment Tucker reappears in the front doorway. She walks slowly to the couch and assumes her former position. Her jaw is set and her eyes are dry. "Are y' done yet?" she asks.

"I've said enough for the moment," Ella replies. "What do you want to say?"

"I've learnt that once y' set yore mind t' somethin', there's little chance o' changin' it. Jes' 'cause I don't agree with y' don't mean I ain't gonna respect yore decision. One time y' tol' me that I sometimes make things all about me. I ain't never fergot that. I figure y' tol' me 'bout yore cancer 'cause y' need somethin' from me. This here is about y' an' what y' want. So tell me, what do y' want from me?"

As Tucker is speaking, Ella smiles warmly even as her tears return and wash her face anew. "I love you, Tucker. I knew if there was one person on the face of this earth who I could count on, it would be you.

"These next few months are not going to be easy or pretty. Toward the end I am not going to be able to take care of myself. I'll need someone to bathe, clothe, and feed me. I want that someone to be you."

Her voice thick with emotion, Tucker replies, "Y' jes' let somebody else try t' do it instead o' me and I'll show 'em th' business end o' my axe handle. Ain't nobody gonna touch y' 'cept me. M' hand'll be th' last hand y' feel on yore face b'fore y' leave this earth. Y' hear me?"

Ella reaches her arms toward Tucker. "Oh, Tucker!"

Tucker welcomes and returns Ella's embrace.

As they hug, Tucker says, "Have y' tol' m' April?"

"That's next," Ella says softly.

CHAPTER TWENTY-SEVEN

Looking out the front window of her house, Ella watches the school bus slowly come to a stop. The double-hinged door opens and April steps off. As is usually the case, her tousled hair has little resemblance to the tamed look it had this morning after Ella fixed it. The blue hair bow that had been on top of April's head is now desperately clinging to the bottom of her long, blond strands, trying to exert at least some effort to stay up. But apparently it is tired after a long day because as April strides toward the house the bow drops softly to the ground.

Ella smiles as she watches her lithe granddaughter step on the porch. She twists toward the front door as the knob turns and April enters.

"Grandmother!" she yells. "I'm home!"

"I'm right here, silly girl," Ella says.

Breaking into a smile, April looks at her and says, "Oh, hi! I didn't see you. Boy, am I starving. That cafeteria lunch today was gross. And it's Friday! No school tomorrow!" She peels off her heavy coat and drops it with her books on the couch as she heads toward the kitchen. "Are there any of those oatmeal cookies left that Tucker gave us when she was here on Tuesday?"

Ella heads toward the kitchen, swept along by the energy of her young charge. "Look in the cookie jar beside the refrigerator."

By the time Ella arrives in the kitchen, April's arm is elbow deep in the green, glass cookie jar. "Easy does it, April. We'll be having supper after a while. I don't want you to ruin your supper."

"But, Grandmother, I'm starving."

Ella's eyebrows peak. "Oh, really? Starving? You are actually starving?"

April looks over her shoulder at her grandmother. "Okay, okay. But I really am very hungry."

Ella holds up three fingers.

"Three," April whines. "How about four? Can't I have four?"

Ella keeps her three fingers in the air. "And I'll fix us some hot chocolate, too. How's that for a compromise?"

The glass lid rattles home as April drops it in place. "Mmmm, that sounds good. It has been cold today."

Ella takes the teakettle off the stove and begins filling it with water from the sink.

"How come you use that to boil water in?" April asks. "Tucker always used a pot to boil water in to make hot cocoa."

"And that works just as well," Ella says. "I just like to hear that whistle when it's ready. It reminds me of when I was a little girl like you and I would visit my grandmother. She always used a teakettle, too."

April takes a generous bite out of one of her cookies. "Youmf falwasyf like—"

"April," Ella says sharply. "Chew and swallow your food before you try to speak. Besides it being bad manners, I can't understand a word you are saying."

April focuses intently on chewing thoroughly and then swallowing her mouthful of cookie. "You sure do like to remember things, don't you? I mean you're always talking about this thing that you remember or that thing you remember."

Ella laughs. "I guess that just comes with getting old. Good memories are like precious jewels. They are to be taken out, admired, and appreciated occasionally, but you don't need to make your life revolve around them."

The teakettle's piercing whistle suddenly demands their attention. April watches thoughtfully as Ella pours the hot water into a mug with hot chocolate mix in the bottom. As the smell of chocolate is released, April inhales deeply. "I love the way chocolate smells."

"What does it remind you of?" Ella asks as she stirs the mixture.

"New Year's Eve," April says immediately.

"Why New Year's Eve?"

"That was the only time we drank it at Tucker's."

"See," Ella says, "that's how memories work. They tie us to our past, reminding us of where we have been."

They move to the table and sit across from each other. Ella puts both hands around her mug and stares into it.

April tips the mug to her mouth and takes a sip. When she sets it down, she has a frothy brown mustache on her lip. Taking another bite of cookie, she quietly studies Ella's face. With the sharp eye of a child, she notices a tear in the corner of Ella's eye. She stops chewing as the tear slowly runs down Ella's cheek and drops into her mug of hot chocolate.

Ella shakes her head in an attempt to snap out of her reverie. When she looks up she sees April staring at her intently. Smiling wanly, she says, "Someone's got a chocolate mustache."

April's pink tongue darts out and swipes her upper lip. Her face is expressionless. She makes no other move. Her keen senses detect a change in the air. Something is different about Ella, but she is not sure what it is. She feels as if a spring in her chest is slowly winding tighter.

"Are you done with your snack?" Ella asks.

April nods, laying her unfinished cookie on the table.

"Let's go sit on the couch and talk."

They go into the living room and assume their familiar positions on the couch. Ella sits on the end by the lamp table, turns toward the middle of the couch, and pulls her feet up in front of her. April sits cross-legged in the middle, facing Ella.

"April," Ella begins, "there is something very important that I have to talk to you about. It's about me and it's about us. You see, I'm sick. Not just like a cold or the flu. It's more serious than that."

Like a rabbit who tries to be hidden simply by not moving, April remains motionless. But her heart beats like the thundering wings of a quail flushed from its nest.

"You remember," Ella continues, "that before I moved out here, before I met all of you, I had been very sick. That's why I didn't have any hair, because I had been treated for it. Do you remember that?"

Ella looks for any response from April but detects nothing. "April?" she prompts. "Do you remember?"

There is the slightest tip of April's head. The spring in April's chest winds tighter with each breath.

"The sickness I had was cancer. I'm sure you've heard of cancer. Since I've lived out here I've been doing fine. Every year I'm stronger and healthier.

"But cancer is a very, very mean disease. It is like a savage and vicious wolf. Sometimes the medicine, like I took, destroys him. But other times it only looks like he's been destroyed. He's actually lying quietly in the weeds, waiting for an opportunity to slip past everyone and attack.

"That's what has happened to me, April. The wolf is back."

Ella pauses to let what she has said sink in and give April an opportunity to react.

Her face still devoid of expression, April says, "Are you going to die?"

Even though she knew this would be part of her explanation to April, Ella stumbles at the calm directness of the question. It takes all her strength to keep looking April in the eye and not look away. "Die?" she says.

"Like my mama, Maisy. Are you going to die?" April's voice lands hard on the word "die." It is the only evidence of emotion that Ella's been able to identify in her granddaughter's reaction.

"Yes, April. I am going to die. The doctor says it may be in the next few months."

April feels the spring in her chest snap. "I'm not surprised," she says calmly. "It's what happens to everyone that I care about. I figured it was only a matter of time before you left me, too. Are we done talking?"

Bewildered, Ella fumbles to find words. "Well . . . I guess . . . I mean, I thought you might . . . is there anything else you'd like to ask or that we need to discuss?"

"No. I want to go to my room."

"Oh, well sure, if that's what you want to do, that'll be fine. I'll be right here if you want to talk later."

The next morning Ella is up early making homemade biscuits and frying ham. She felt guilty all night about allowing April, at her request, to skip supper and stay in her room. Even though she thought it might be good for April to have some alone time, Ella woke up full of doubts about that decision. Cooking a big breakfast would be a good way for them both to start afresh. Normally just the smell of breakfast would have April scurrying excitedly into the kitchen.

"April! Breakfast will be ready soon. Hot biscuits with butter and honey and ham and eggs are looking forward to greeting you."

After she scrapes the scrambled eggs into a bowl and takes the biscuits out of the oven, she calls again, "April! Come on before it gets . . ." Her voice trails off. Unconsciously dropping her pot holders to the floor, Ella looks toward April's closed door. She walks stiffly to April's room. Her normal pallor of the past few months takes on a whiter shade of pale.

With dread, she lightly taps on the door. "April?" Putting her ear to the door, she hopes for a reply. In response to the eerie silence, she slowly opens the door. She gasps as her hand flies to her mouth. Her eyes bug out. She stifles a cry.

Ella tries to absorb the visual assault that has punched her. April's room looks as if a rabid Tasmanian devil has run amok in it. The sheers on her window hang in tatters. Foam stuffing from her bed pillows is scattered throughout the room like so much popcorn. Her mattress is completely bare, the sheets and comforter piled in a heap beside the bed.

Ella steps cautiously into the room for a closer inspection. It is then that she sees all of April's dolls lying in a heap in one corner of the room. Ella squats before the discarded, lifeless heap. Suddenly she realizes that they have had their heads ripped off.

Looking to her left, she sees the heads on the floor, lined against the wall. In horror, Ella discovers all the dolls' eyes have been torn off or gouged out.

But nowhere is there any sign of April.

CHAPTER TWENTY-EIGHT

So Miss Ella said fer y' t' come spend th' night with me? Is that what happened?" Tucker looks at April out of the corner of her eye while spooning steaming oatmeal into a bowl. "An' I was done in bed when y' got here, so y' jes' slept on th' couch? Is that it? Don't none o' that make sense t' me." She fills another bowl with oatmeal.

Sitting one bowl in front of the seated, expressionless April, Tucker sits across from her and dips a spoonful of oatmeal from her own bowl. "Mmmm, nothin' like hot oatmeal on a cold mornin' like this. Y' better dig in." She motions toward April's bowl.

April's uncombed hair gives her the appearance of a scarecrow. She lifts her spoon as if it were as heavy as a shovel. She drops it in the bowl and watches it slide slowly into the thick oatmeal like a man drowning in quicksand. Her open mouth receives the loaded spoon, but she doesn't swallow. Her eyes are vacant.

"Ain't y' gonna say nothin'?" Tucker asks. "Y' gotta say somethin', child. Tell me what happened."

April looks up at Tucker. A light flickers in her eyes. She opens her mouth to speak but just as quickly closes it. The light is gone. Her eyes look flat and cold.

Tucker feels a shudder run up her spine. She chews thoughtfully on her bottom lip. "Well, this ain't gitten us nowhere. We need t' walk down t' Miss Ella's an' talk with her." She reaches to take April's bowl of oatmeal. As quickly as a steel trap closing, April's hand clamps Tucker's hand to the table.

The suddenness of April's move startles Tucker. But she keeps her initial reaction in check. Rather than twisting April's arm and pinning her, Tucker keeps very still. She looks from her hand to April's face.

April does not return the look. She seems focused on something, but it is not in Tucker's house.

In a soft, calm voice Tucker says, "That's it, baby. Whatever's troublin' m' April, y' can tell ol' Tucker. I can tell it's 'bout Miss Ella. It's okay. I'm—" Tucker stops in midsentence as realization finds its way into her. "She tol'ja, didn't she? 'Bout her cancer."

April's hand flexes like a claw and her nails dig into the back of Tucker's hand. But Tucker shows no reaction.

"It's a helluva thing, ain't it, honey? I ain't sure what t' think 'bout it m'self. An' I'm sad fer y', April. I ain't gonna say it ain't fair, 'cause life ain't supposed t' be fair. It's jes' a bad, bad thing. But here's what we're gonna do. We're gonna git through this—you, me, August, Smiley Carter—we gonna git through it. An' we're gonna do it by not makin' this 'bout us an' our hurt. We're gonna be there fer Ella. She's been there fer us plenty o' times, ain't she?" She places her free hand on top of April's hand. She lets the natural weight of her hand take the fearful fight out of April's.

April's hand slowly relaxes and flattens in between Tucker's two thick hands. She looks up at Tucker, tears pooling in her eyes.

Tucker sees recognition in April's eyes. "Yes, m' April, we're gonna do this. We're gonna do it t'gether. Ain't we?"

As if there were siphons in her tear ducts, the tears in April's eyes disappear. She nods her head.

"Good girl. Now come over here an' give ol' Tucker a hug."

April frees her hand from Tucker's and walks around the table. She opens her thin arms as she approaches Tucker and wraps them around her thick neck as Tucker envelopes her in her strong arms.

"Now don't y' think we need t' go to Miss Ella's? I'll bet she's out o' 'er mind worryin' 'bout where y' are."

At that moment, Ella comes bursting through Tucker's front door. "Tucker!" she yells. "Tucker, where are you? It's April. I can't—" As she makes her way to the kitchen, she spies Tucker and April embracing and stops in her tracks. "Oh, thank God you are all right."

April moves behind Tucker's chair and looks at Ella over Tucker's shoulder.

Ella is taken aback by April's reaction.

Ignoring April, Tucker says casually, "Come in an' have a seat, Ella. We's jes' been talkin' 'bout you. April came up here t' be sure I knowed 'bout y' havin' cancer." She sees the confused expression on Ella's face and, catching her eye, Tucker winks at her and nods at an empty chair.

Ella decides to follow Tucker's lead and sits at the table.

"So," Tucker says, "like I was sayin', I tol' April that y' an' I had done talked 'bout y' havin' cancer and ever'thing. An' I tol' her that we was all gonna git through this t'gether. I said she shoulda tol' y' 'bout comin' up here an' that you'd be scared an' worried when y' woke up and couln't find her. She said she was real sorry 'bout that. She didn't think 'bout that."

Ella looks at April peeping over Tucker's shoulder. As soon as their eyes meet, April slowly moves out of sight behind Tucker's head.

"Well," Ella says, "I'm just glad she's all right. That's all that matters to me. Really. Nothing else matters. We all do and say things when we're upset that we later regret. Don't we, Tucker?"

Tucker now finds herself attempting to follow Ella's lead. "Well, course that happens sometimes. I once got mad at a chicken 'cause it pecked m' sore toe. I snatched it up, wrung its neck, an' cooked it fer supper." Shaking her head, she adds, "Always wished I hadn't done that. It didn't mean no harm. It was jes' bein' a chicken."

Having watched Tucker wring the neck of chickens with the conscience of an executioner, Ella is bemused by this tale of remorse. She has a vision of the hapless, headless bird flying through the air, landing with an explosion of feathers, and running pell-mell around the yard. She laughs and says, "I'll bet that was the most surprised chicken on the planet—for about two seconds."

Tucker smiles. "Poor thing was jes' mindin' 'er own business when all of a sudden I grabbed 'er." As she finishes her sentence Tucker deftly reaches behind her and grabs April. April squeals in surprise. "Looks like I done caught me another chicken, Ella!" She pulls the wriggling April to her lap and begins tickling her.

As April explodes with laughter, Ella says, "She sounds just like a chicken cackling!"

Tucker stands up and holds the wriggling, protesting April upside down. "Grab a pot, Ella! This chicken's goin' in th' stew pot fer supper!"

CHAPTER TWENTY-NINE

December 18

Tucker arrives at Ella's house for her daily visit to check on her friend. As has become her custom, she enters without knocking. Ella is not in her familiar place on the couch. Tucker hears rattling dishes in the kitchen. As she walks into the kitchen, she sees April at the sink washing dishes.

"Mornin', April. Where's Ella?" Her hope is that April will actually tell her where Ella is. Since learning from Ella of her impending death, April has rarely spoken.

April turns her head to look at Tucker. Her eyes are red rimmed and her nose looks like a raspberry.

"What's th' matter, child? Where's Ella?"

April nods her head toward Ella's bedroom.

Tucker steps quietly to the door and taps lightly. "Ella?" she says softly.

Ella's weak voice answers, "Come in, Tucker."

Opening the door, Tucker sees Ella lying in her bed, her hand extended toward her.

"Come here, Tucker." She pats the bed beside her. "Sit down."

The mattress sags as Tucker settles on the edge of the bed. She notices Ella's pasty complexion and the fatigue in her eyes. Gently touching the side of Ella's face, she says, "What's th' matter, pretty lady? Y' been drinkin' too much o' that special eggnog I made up fer y'?"

A faint smile crosses Ella's face. "Ever since you surprised me with your homemade cold medicine, I'm extra cautious with what you bring me." Shaking her head, she says, "But it's not the eggnog. I just don't feel like myself today. I tried to get up this morning to fix breakfast, but was out of breath from walking to the bathroom." She places her hand on Tucker's. "I think it's time."

Tucker's eyebrows go up. "Time?"

"Yes, time for you to move in with me. I don't think I'm going to be able to manage things without you being here all the time to help me."

"Yes, ma'am, sweet sister. We both knowed this was a'comin'. I jes' been waitin' on th' word from y'. I'll go git m' things in a bit and move in th' spare bedroom like y' planned. But what can I do fer y' right now? Are y' hungry 'r thirsty?"

"Oh, Tucker, you should have seen April this morning. When I wasn't up like usual she came into my room to check on me. I told her I was a little tired this morning and she'd have to fix herself something to eat. Well, the little trouper came back after a bit with a bowl of cream of rice and a glass of juice on a tray. It was the sweetest thing.

"So, I've had some breakfast. Why don't you go ahead and get your things."

Before Tucker answers, the sound of heavy footsteps approaches Ella's door. The large bulk of Smiley Carter fills the open doorway.

"Is this here what you white folks call a 'hen party'? Or can a handsome black man come in?" His signature smile practically glows in the dim light.

"Oh good Lord," Tucker moans. "If there was a handsome black man in this house, I'd sure 'nough invite 'im in. It's jes' too bad there ain't one."

Carter grabs his chest and leans against the door frame. "Shot again by a sharp arrow from the quiver of Tucker."

Ella manages a feeble laugh.

Carter walks to the bedside. "So, is the madam of the house taking the day off?"

Tucker stands up and faces him. They look each other in the eye. She closes her eyes and gives her head a slight shake. Opening her eyes, she raises her eyebrows to be sure Carter has understood her message.

He nods at her and says in a loud voice, "Well, that's about what I figured. Miss Ella always did want a black butler waiting on her out here. Guess I'll have to find me one of them tuxedos to wear."

Tucker moves beside him and says softly, "I'm fixin' t' go git m' things an' move in."

Carter steps around her and bows deeply. "At your service, Miss Ella."

Tucker calls from the doorway, "Ella, I'll be back in a bit. Don't let this idiot trouble y'. Send 'im out t' count th' rocks in th' driveway, if y' need t' git 'im outta yore hair."

"Don't you worry about me," Ella says. "I know how to handle ruffians like him."

Tucker walks into the kitchen and finds April on all fours, halfway inside the oven. "April! What the—?"

Startled, April backs out of the oven. She has on oversized Playtex gloves and is holding a dirty rag in each hand. With a look bordering on panic, she points to the inside of the oven.

Tucker grunts as she bends down to look inside the oven. "Sweet April, it ain't that bad. Don't worry 'bout it. It ain't important. Why don't y' come with me t' th' house? I gotta git me some things an' bring 'em down here. I'm gonna be livin' with y' and Ella fer a while."

April's eyes widen and her shoulders sag. She looks at the open oven and then back to Tucker. She leans toward the oven and turns away from Tucker. As she starts to crawl back into the black cavern, Tucker gently lifts her.

"Tucker needs y', too. I'll need help gittin' th' house ready t' leave empty, in case it turns cold." She pinches the empty fingers of April's oversized gloves and slowly pulls. "Let's git these off."

April reluctantly acquiesces to Tucker's will.

When they go out the front door, they discover August walking toward the house. He breaks into a wide grin when he sees Tucker. "There you are! I just got through walking up to the house to visit and couldn't find you anywhere."

He sidles up to Tucker and she puts her arm around his shoulders. Squeezing him tightly, she says, "Y' one handsome young man, y' know it?"

His only response is to beam at her. Glancing at April, he says, "Where are you two going?"

"We's headed t' th' house t' git me some things t' bring back down here. I'm gonna be stayin' down here fer a while." She ignores his puzzled expression and begins walking toward the road. "Come on, you two, let's git busy."

Inside Ella's house, Carter sits on the side of Ella's bed, holding and patting her hand. "So, what can ol' Carter do for you?"

"Just knowing you are ready and willing is enough for me. This is a new chapter for us, but it is a familiar chapter for me. I'm feeling bad today, but I'll perk back up again. That's the way it goes. There's no way to predict what kind of day I'll have. I just don't like April having to take care of herself. That's why I told Tucker it is time for her to move in with us. And I need her here because it will get worse."

A solitary tear escapes from behind Carter's brave facade. It leaves a shiny trail as it rolls down his face and then drops on his chest, close to the heart from which it came. "Here's what I don't understand," he says. "Why won't you let the doctor give you some medicine that will at least ease you? I know they can do that."

"Because," Ella replies, "all that does is put me in a fog. I'll be here, but I won't know or remember anything. I won't be able to make sensible conversation." Gripping his hand tightly, she says, "I want to live right up to the time I die. Can you understand that?"

"When you put it that way, there ain't much a man can say back. You want to go on your terms. I respect that."

Ella smiles. "Good. I'm relieved. Now, how about fixing me a cup of hot tea?"

Carter stands up. With a twinkle in his eye, he says, "Yes, ma'am, Misses Overseer. I go fetch that right quick fer ye." He ends by bowing deeply.

When he straightens up, a small bed pillow strikes him in the face.

CHAPTER THIRTY

December 23

Tucker takes the dish towel from April. "Thankye fer helpin' with th' breakfast dishes. Y' are one good hand when it comes t' cleanin' things. I ain't never seen anythin' quite like it."

April looks blankly at Tucker.

"I'm gonna go sit on th' couch an' look at some more pictures in Ella's magazines while she's restin'. Y' wanta come sit with me an' look? Or maybe read some t' me?"

April's face remains inscrutable.

Tucker pats her on the head. "Well, y' can do whatever y' want."

An hour later, Tucker hears the sound of a car door closing outside. She rises stiffly from the couch and walks to the front door. When she opens the door Sheriff Ron Harris is standing there with his hand raised in position to knock.

Startled, he blurts, "Oh, hey there, Tucker." He looks dumbly at his fist still hanging in the air. Lowering it to his side, he says, "You're quick on the draw. Didn't even have time to knock."

Tucker crosses her arms across her chest. "Miss Ella ain't takin' no visitors. In case y' ain't heard, she's not well."

Harris pushes his Stetson to the back of his head. Looking at his boots, he says, "Yeah, I heard. Man, that is just the worst thing. She's such a good lady and has been doing so well. Cancer—I hate it. It's what killed my mother."

He is silent for a few moments. Suddenly he looks up from his reverie. "But she's not why I'm here. I've come to talk to you, Tucker. Can we step out into the yard, away from the house? I don't want anyone to hear this conversation."

Without waiting for a response, he walks toward his patrol car. Tucker follows several paces behind him.

When he turns back to face her, his expression is grim. "The first thing I'm going to say is that I don't make laws, I just enforce them. Even if I don't like them, I still have to do my job. And right now I think I'd rather have any job in the world than to be the sheriff of Weakley County and have to deliver this news to you."

Tucker takes the slightest step backward. Her eyes blink rapidly. She feels her face flush.

Reaching into his hip pocket, Harris pulls out a folded piece of paper. He looks at it thoughtfully. "There's no easy way to do this, Tucker. And I don't guess there could be a worse time to do it." He holds up the paper. "This is an eviction notice for you. It says that one month from today you must be removed from your premises. Your place will then be sold at public auction on the courthouse steps to pay for back taxes. There will be no more delays or further notices. This is it."

He stretches his hand with the paper in it toward Tucker.

In a flash Tucker slaps his hand, knocking the paper to the ground.

Suddenly the passenger door of the patrol car flies open and Deputy King springs from it in a dead run.

Tucker turns toward him and lowers her shoulder.

"Stop!" Harris yells.

Like a trained German shepherd, his deputy stops in his tracks and looks to his boss for further instructions.

"I told you not to get out of the car unless I called you. Now get back in there! I'm handling this fine."

Keeping his eyes on Tucker, the deputy walks backward toward the car and lowers himself into his seat. The door closes quietly.

Bending over to pick up the paper, Harris says, "I'm sorry, Tucker. He means well. Just too damn gung ho sometimes."

"I ain't scared o' him 'r you either."

"I know that, Tucker." Harris takes a deep breath. "Look, I don't mean to add insult to injury, but I'm required to hand this paper to you."

When she doesn't offer to take it, Harris lays it on her folded arms.

"It will be my duty to be at your house one month from today, January 23, to escort you from your house, if you are still there."

"An' jes' where is it that y' aim t' take me? Where will I live?"

Harris squares his Stetson hat on his head. "That's not part of my concern. My job is to be sure you vacate the premises. Maybe you could live in the projects."

"Hmpf, over my dead body. I ain't gonna live with all that white trash an' them nig—black people."

Harris's eyes narrow. "What are you saying?"

"Jes' what I said. I ain't gonna live in a place like that. Besides, I've lived out here in th' country m' whole life. It would smother me t' live in town." Shaking her head, she adds, "No, sir. It ain't gonna happen."

Earnestly, Harris says, "Listen to me. I don't want there to be any trouble when January 23 gets here. You just have to accept that this is the way it's going to be."

With an unblinking stare, Tucker says, "We'll see 'bout that. We'll see."

Harris considers a reply and then turns and walks to his patrol car. Just before he lowers himself into the driver's seat, he says to her again, "January 23."

Without waiting to watch him drive off, Tucker turns and goes back into Ella's house. She goes to Ella's bedroom and opens the door a crack.

"Is that you, Tucker?" says a weak voice.

Tucker opens the door wider and walks to Ella's bed. "Yes, it's me. I was jes' checkin' on y'. Y' need anything?"

"I thought I heard voices outside. Who was it?"

"It was jes' the sheriff. He come by t' see how y' was doin'. I wouldn't let 'im come in. Said y' was restin'."

"How kind of him. He's a good man, that Ron Harris."

CHAPTER THIRTY-ONE

December 25

Y' kids hurry up," Tucker barks. "It's gittin' close to mealtime an' when Ella comes out I want that Christmas tree fixed up like she done it 'erself."

April is on her knees beside a cardboard box.

"Hand me that sparkly rope," August says. "Miss Ella always wrapped it 'round the tree from top to bottom."

April stands up and hands him the golden tree garland.

August easily reaches the top of the tree and slowly walks around it while draping the trimming on the tree branches.

Smiley Carter walks from the kitchen to the dining table carrying two steaming bowls. He glances into the living room. "You kids is doing a great job on that tree. Ella's going to be so excited when she sees it. But they's something missing."

April lifts a thick mass of white tissue paper from the box. She carefully unfolds it to reveal a cut-glass ornamental star. A broad smile spreads across her face. She touches August's arm and hands it to him.

"Oh, that's what was missing," Carter says.

August smiles. "This is what makes this tree the most special tree. I've never seen a star that looks like this one." He places it on the very top of the tree.

The star catches every light on the tree and in the house and sends them through a prism, creating rainbow-edged colors on the ceiling and wall. As Tucker carries a platter of ham to the table, she, too, stops to admire the spectacle.

Carter whistles low. "You're right, August. I don't believe they's another star like that in the world. That's Miss Ella's star." As he speaks, tears begin their downward migration from his sorrow-filled eyes.

Tucker sets the ham on the table and notices Carter crying. "Listen to me, Smiley Carter!" she hisses. "Y' ain't gonna cry on this night. This here is gonna be a good night, a night o' happy memories. An' if'n y' can't control yoreself, then y' need t' step into th' backyard until y' git hold o' yoreself. Y' hear me?"

Wiping his eyes with his bandanna, Carter says, "You's right. An' I'm tryin'. Lord knows I'm tryin'."

"Well, try harder. An' th' same goes fer y' two kids, too. Y' understand?"

"Yes, ma'am," August replies.

April nods her head.

"Good." Tucker surveys the table. "I think ever'thing's ready. Where th' devil is Shady Green? I thought y' said he was comin'."

"That's what he told me," Carter replies. "I offered to let him ride with me, but he said he'd walk over on his own. But let's not wait on him. Knowing him, he forgot about the meal."

"Then ever'body gather roun' th' table, an' I'll go bring Ella in."

Carter and the children take positions behind their usual chairs.

After a moment, the door to Ella's bedroom opens and Tucker leads her by her elbow through the opening.

Ella's slippers make a scuffing noise as she shuffles beside Tucker. The red Christmas dress she wore last year looks three sizes too big for her disappearing body. Gone is the pasty complexion. It is replaced by a greenish-yellow cast. Her cheeks are sunken, making her naturally high cheekbones look startlingly sharp.

Carter squeezes the back of his chair until it creaks.

August's mouth stands open.

April stares at the table.

"Well, ain't nobody gonna say how purty our special lady looks?" Tucker asks into the silence of the room.

Clearing his throat, Carter says, "Now there's a striking woman if ever I seen one. Ain't she, August?" He slaps his son on the side of the arm.

Startled, August stammers, "Uh . . . yeah . . . sure . . . she's . . ."

"I knowed what you mean." Carter attempts to cover the awkward moment. "It's hard to find words, isn't it?"

Ella smiles faintly. "You are both the two worst liars in the county, maybe in West Tennessee. I've got a mirror, you know. I can see what I look like." Then she notices the Christmas tree. A small cry escapes her and her free hand goes to her mouth. "It's perfect." Looking to August and April, she says, "You two did it, didn't you? I can tell. You both have an artist's eye and touch. I couldn't have done better myself."

"Come on, now," Tucker says. "Let's git y' to th' table so y' don't git too tired."

When Ella takes her seat, a grimace creases her face.

Everyone else settles into their chairs.

Ella rests her hands, palms up, on the table. She looks at each one and they understand her meaning. Everyone takes the hand of the person next to them.

"You want me to offer the blessing?" Carter asks.

"Not this time. I want to do it." She closes her eyes and lowers her head.

They all imitate her.

There are several moments of silence. So much so that Tucker peeks out of one eye to be sure Ella is okay.

"Dear, sweet Lord above," Ella begins. Her deep breaths indicate the effort it is costing to speak aloud. "Thank you for letting me . . . see this night and for surrounding . . . me with people I love . . . and who love me . . . The only thing . . . that is going to be sweeter than this . . . is when I'm home with you . . . Please . . . bless and watch over . . . these special people . . . after I'm gone . . . Now, for this . . . bountiful feast . . . we're about to partake of . . . we give you thanks . . . Amen."

She lifts her head only to see everyone else's still bowed. "That's all people," Ella says. "Let's eat."

With her head still bowed, Tucker lifts a napkin to her face. "I got somethin' in m' eye, I think."

Carter says, "I think I need to step into the backyard and check on something."

Ella hits the table with the flat of her hand.

Tucker's and Carter's heads jerk up.

August jumps.

April turns and looks at Ella.

"Listen to me, all of you," Ella says. "Stop pretending . . . Stop pretending you're not sad . . . or unhappy or upset . . . or angry or scared . . . There is nothing wrong . . . with feeling hurt and . . . crying about it . . . It's a sign you care . . . It won't upset me . . . to see you cry . . . Sometimes I cry, too . . . It's okay. So stop all this . . . playacting . . . Let's be honest . . . with each other . . . for these last weeks . . . Agreed?"

She looks at Carter. He places his hand on top of hers. "Ain't you something? Remarkable, that's what you are. Agreed."

She turns to Tucker. "Agreed," Tucker says.

Next she looks at August. His eyes are red rimmed. "Yes, ma'am."

Then she looks at April, who is smiling. "Yes, Grandmother. It's okay to be upset."

Suddenly there is a thud on the front porch and a knock on the door.

"Who in th' world is that?" Tucker asks. "Here it is Christmas night. Go see who it is, Carter."

Carter gets out of his chair and goes to the door. Opening it, a voice is heard, "Ehwee Isswass! Ehwee Isswass!"

"Shady Green!" August exclaims.

Carter swings the door open wide.

Shady Green strides in, his guitar in its pillow-case carried dutifully at his side. He has on a brown plaid, double-knit sport coat that is too big. One of the front pockets is hanging on by a few threads. Around his neck is an extra wide, purple-striped tie that fills the opening of the front of his jacket. Rounding out his ensemble is a pair of dark blue, double-knit pants. When Shady Green sees everyone gathered at the table, he exclaims, "Ehwee Isswass, evry-bah-ee!"

He beams at the chorus of greetings his friends throw in his direction.

After the meal is finished, Tucker says, "Let's go in th' livin' room where Ella can lay on th' couch an' be easy."

Before anyone makes a move to leave the table, Shady Green looks at April and says, "Ah ooo 'eady foh r sur' rise?"

Puzzled expressions appear on everyone's face except April's. She smiles, nods her head, and goes to her bedroom.

Shady Green gets up from his chair and says, "Ehss oh eh'erbah'ee," and waves for them to follow him to the living room.

Carter helps Ella up from her chair and he and Tucker assist her to the couch.

"What in the world are you up to, Shady Green?" Ella asks.

Unwrapping his guitar, Shady displays a snaggletooth grin and says, "Ooo 'ust 'ait an' see."

Everyone watches him strap on his guitar. They don't see April reenter from her bedroom. Carrying Ella's Autoharp case, she walks straight to Shady. Sitting it at his feet, she opens the case and removes the instrument. She then sits in a chair beside him and lays the Autoharp in her lap.

April looks at her stunned audience and then looks to Shady. "Ready?" she says.

Shady nods vigorously.

April immediately begins strumming a quick-paced rhythm. After a couple of beats, Shady strums along with her. She looks up at him and nods.

He looks at Ella and says, "Foh ooo 'iss, Ehwuh."

Then Shady Green opens his mouth and, with enunciation that is as clear as Charles Kuralt, begins singing:

Back up in the mountains in that old hometown of mine
There's not a brighter time of year than that of Christmastime
The bells in the little church they all begin to chime
Telling all for miles around, Rejoice! It's Christmastime!

Christmas bells are ringing; I hear the times so sweet
The carolers are singing; I hear them in the street
Outside the white snow falling; inside my heart I find
A world of joy and peace on earth back home at Christmastime.

A candle in each window; they give a golden glow

While out among the shimmering pines lights sparkle in the
snow
And through the lonely mountaintops the wind's shrill echoes
cry
For peace on earth good will toward men and faith that will
not die.

High above our little town so bright to be so far
There shines upon the whole wide world His gift our guiding
star
Everyone in each home can feel a peace sublime
And know the joy the Yuletide brings to all at Christmastime.

The last tones of the song hang in the air, not willing to let go. Everyone in the room looks as if they've had a spell cast on them by a wizard who has turned them into stone.

Finally, Carter shakes his head as if coming out of a deep sleep. He rubs his eyes and says, "If I had not been here to see and hear what I just heard, I would say it was impossible."

August says, "April, that was awesome playing! And Shady Green, you were unbelievable! That was the coolest thing I've ever seen!"

Tucker rubs her chin. "I ain't got no idea how y' done what y' jes' done, Shady Green. I jes' don't know."

Her face wet with tears, Ella says, "It is a Christmas miracle. We've all just witnessed . . . a miracle." She reaches her arms toward Shady Green. "Come here."

Shady Green walks to her and kneels like a knight before his queen.

Ella puts her hands on his face, pulls him toward her, and kisses him on his forehead. "That may have been the most special Christmas present anyone has ever given me."

Shady pulls back from her. Tears are dripping off his hawk-like nose. "'Ank ooo, Ehwuh."

CHAPTER THIRTY-TWO

January 4

Tucker stomps her feet as she enters the back door of Ella's house. The vibrations dislodge clumps of snow from the cleats in her boots and scatter them across the floor. She unfastens her heavy, blue jean jumper and, opening it, shakes snow off her shoulders and back. The heat of her bare head has melted all the snow that had fallen on it, so steam seems to be coming off her head like the smoke from a steam locomotive. Like a dog after its bath, Tucker gives her head a vigorous shake.

After hanging up her coat and removing her boots, she cups her hands to her mouth and blows into them. She makes her way to the stove and turns on the teakettle.

Going to Ella's bedroom, Tucker eases quietly through the door.

Ella is sitting up in bed reading. She hears the floor creak and turns to see Tucker. "Your nose is as red as Rudolph's! It must be really cold outside. How much snow is there?"

Tucker rubs her hands vigorously and then puts them under her armpits. "Must be 'round ten degrees an', dependin' on where y' measure, I'd say a good foot o' snow."

"Are your animals okay?"

"Yep. All o' 'em is bedded up in th' barn. Got water an' feed. So they'll be fine. Y' seem t' be havin' a good mornin'."

"Yes, I am. I'm not hurting as much and had a decent sleep last night." Keeping her hand on the page she was reading, Ella closes the book.

Tucker notices the cover. "Y' been readin' a lot outta that recently. What's in there that makes y' want t' read it so much?"

Ella looks down at the worn, black leather cover. Opening it again to the saved page, she says, "It was my mother's Bible. I'm going through it, reading the passages that she had underlined. Sometimes I can hear her reading it to me. Then, other times, it gives me some insight into who she was. But mainly I find the words in it very comforting."

The whistling teakettle interrupts them. Tucker heads to the kitchen. "I'll be right back with some hot tea."

"Tucker," Ella says. "This will sound silly, but you know what I'd really like? I'd like some snow cream. That's all I've been thinking about since it started snowing."

"Lordy mercy, girl," Tucker exclaims. "That sounds like fun. I wouldn't never thought 'bout y' an' me sharin' a bowl. I'll fix some up an' be right back."

After a bit, Tucker returns carrying two bowls with spoons in them. She hands a bowl to Ella, then grabs the rocking chair and pulls it closer to the bed.

"Mmmm, this is so good," Ella says. "You put something in it besides milk, sugar, and vanilla. I can't quite figure out what it is."

"I like t' put jes' th' tiniest amount o' nutmeg."

"That's it! Yes, I can taste it now. Delicious."

"Be careful an' don't eat too fast. It'll make yore head feel like it's gonna explode."

155

After they finish eating, Tucker sets their bowls on the floor. She slowly rocks in her chair. After a few moments she motions toward the Bible lying beside Ella and says, "So read me one o' yore favorites in there."

Ella picks it up and says, "Oh my, that's hard to choose." She opens it in the middle and flips a few pages. "But here's one, one that was probably the first passage I ever memorized as a child.

The Lord is my shepherd;
I shall not want.
He maketh me to lie down in green pastures:
He leadeth me beside still waters.
He restoreth my soul.
He leadeth me in the paths of righteousness for his name's sake.
Yea though I walk through the valley of the shadow of death,
I will fear no evil:
For thou art with me;
Thy rod and Thy staff, they comfort me.
Thou preparest a table before me in the presence of mine enemies:
Thou anointest my head with oil;
My cup runneth over.
Surely goodness and mercy shall follow me all the days of my life:
And I will dwell in the house of the Lord forever.

"That sounds purty," Tucker says. "Is that why y' ain't scared?"
"Scared?"
"Y' know—scared t' die. T' be walkin' through this here valley o' th' shadow o' death. Y' don't seemed scared 'bout it at all."
Ella looks thoughtfully at her friend. "I'm not scared because I know I'm going to a better place and either God or his angels will escort me there. Living here has only been a brief stopover on my way to an eternal home."

Tucker's eyes blink rapidly as she listens to Ella's explanation.

Ella starts turning pages on the right-hand side of her Bible. She stops and puts her finger on what she is looking at. "Listen to this one, Tucker. It just sounds so exciting and comforting, too.

"'Let not your heart be troubled: ye believe in God, believe also in me.

"'In my Father's house are many mansions: if it were not so, I would have told you.

"'I go to prepare a place for you. And if I go and prepare a place for you, I will come again and receive you unto myself; that where I am, there ye may be also.'"

Tucker slams both palms on the arms of her chair. Scowling, she says, "I don't see how y' can be all 'bout this God thing. Look what he's doin' t' y', an' y' one o' th' best people I ever knowed. An' I ain't never seen nothin' he ever done fer me, either." Her face reddens and tears form in her eyes. "I can remember a time when I was little that I b'lieved in God. But th' longer I lived in th' hell o' my life, I decided there couldn't be no God, not if he let happen what happened t' me."

"Oh, my dear, that's not right," Ella replies. "Now, don't misunderstand me; I certainly don't have how life works all figured out, but here's something I do. God is responsible for all the good in my life. As for all the bad? Sometimes it's because I make bad choices, but most of the time it's because of our archenemy, Satan."

"Satan, huh. I'll find out fer m'self one day when I meet 'im in hell."

Ella frowns. "What do you mean by that?"

"Jes' what I said. I'll meet 'im in hell one day 'cause that's where I'll go when I'm done livin'. I been headin' fer hell ever since I's sixteen years old." Tucker sees the shock on Ella's face. "Lookee here, Ella. If'n there is a heaven, then there ain't no doubt in m' mind that you're gonna be there on th' front row. You're a good woman with a good heart. Y' deserve heaven. But me? You know what I've done in th' past. I deserve t' go t' hell. It's jes' that simple."

Ella shakes her head. "No, no, no, you've got it all wrong. The same way I had it all wrong for such a long time." She closes her eyes and lays her head back.

Tucker quickly gets out of her chair and moves to Ella's bedside. "Damn me! Me an' my mouth. I shouldn'a got y' so upset an' wore out. Y' need t' lay down in them covers fer a while an' rest, maybe take y' a nap." She puts her arms under the covers and slides them under Ella's back. She shifts Ella until she is lying flat, then gently fluffs her pillow. Placing the back of her hand against Ella's cheek, she says, "Better?"

Ella opens her eyes. "Yes, better. But we aren't through talking about this, you hear?"

"Whatever y' say," Tucker replies.

Ella grasps Tucker's sleeve. "No, I'm serious. We will talk again."

"Okay, okay. We'll talk again. But not right now. You're gonna rest right now. And I'm serious."

Ella releases her grip on Tucker. "Good. That's good." The next instant she falls asleep.

CHAPTER THIRTY-THREE

January 8

W hat does it mean?" Smiley Carter asks.

"Hell if I know!" Tucker snaps. "All I know is she ain't been awake hardly any fer th' last four days. Jes' lays there breathin' real slow an' shallow."

"I spoke to her once when she was awake yesterday," Carter says. "But it was like she didn't even know who I was. I think she thought I was her daddy. She said, 'I'm coming soon.'"

"I ain't never been 'round nobody who was dyin'. Is this how it is? I mean, is she fixin' t' die anytime now?"

Carter stares into the black coffee in his cup and sees his troubled reflection. "I seen it happen lots of different ways. Sometimes people lingers for weeks and months even though it seems like every breath is they last one. Then, some folks nearly die but will suddenly perk up. Makes everyone think they's all better. But they've only woke up to tell everybody good-bye. And suddenly their light goes out, just like that." He snaps his fingers for emphasis.

Tucker takes her glasses off and rubs her eyes.

"I know you got to be tired, Tucker. Why don't you take a nap? I'll wake you if anything happens or changes."

Shaking her head, Tucker says, "No, sir. I promised Ella I'd be here fer 'er. An' that's what I aim t' do."

She puts her glasses back on and crosses her arms. "But there's somethin' I needs t' ask y' about. It's somethin' Ella an' me discussed a few days ago."

Carter's eyebrows go up. "I'm here and listening."

"I'm guessin' y' know how it was with m' daddy an' me an' what all he did t' me when I was growin' up." She pauses.

Carter's expression turns grim and he nods.

"Well, I tol' Ella all 'bout it. Then she tol' me 'bout 'er an' Judge Jack an' all th' hell he put 'er through when they was married. She said she finally come t' th' place she decided she needed t' fergive 'im fer all he done. But th' kicker was when she tol' me I needed t' fergive m' daddy fer what he done t' me." Unfolding her arms, she lays them on the table and asks, "So wha'j' think 'bout that?"

Carter gives a low whistle. He throws his head up in the air like a horse going through an unfamiliar gate. "You've hit a mighty troublesome spot in ol' Smiley Carter. Mighty troublesome." He shakes his head slowly.

Placing his folded hands on the table, he looks at Tucker and says, "I knows what the good book says about forgiveness: 'Forgive me of my trespasses as I have forgiven those who have trespassed against me.' Yes, sir, that's what it says. So I believe it's true—we have to forgive, if we want to be forgiven. And when you've lived the kind of life that I have, you definitely want to have God's forgiveness on your side. Without it I'd be riding on a fast train to hell."

Tucker frowns. "Well, who in th' world did y' have t' fergive? Y' come from a good family. It wadn't nothin' like mine."

Carter stares at her openmouthed. "You serious, ain't you? You don't have no idea what growing up black was like, do you? Who did I have to forgive? What about the KKK that hung my uncle and then dragged him behind their car? What about a country that made me use bathrooms, water fountains, and restaurants separate from white folks? And what about a country that took my son from me and sent him to the hellhole called Viet Nam, while the rich white kids got to stay safe at home? And they's the drunk white doctor that let my wife die when our son was born. What about him?" As Carter speaks, his voice rises in volume and pitch with each question. At the last statement his fist hammers on the table.

Tucker blinks rapidly.

Carter wipes sweat beads off his upper lip with his bare hand. "Trust me, I've had plenty of opportunity to practice forgiveness." He gets up from the table to pour himself another cup of coffee out of the pot on the stove.

Walking back to the table, he sits down and continues. "What I figured out was that me carrying around all my anger and hatred was turning me into someone I didn't like. And when you don't like yourself, you live a pitiful life. The only way out of that hole was for me to start forgiving some folks."

Tucker's hands close into fists. Through gritted teeth she says, "But m' daddy don't deserve t' be forgiven. Anybody what done what he did don't deserve nothin' but killin'."

Carter makes a sucking sound with his teeth. "No doubt about that. Here's the thing, though. Forgiving somebody ain't because they deserve it." He taps his chest. "It's something you do for your heart, not theirs."

Tucker shakes her head. "Now, y' ain't makin' no sense at all."

Carter gives her an understanding smile. "I know. I felt the same way when my preacher talked to me about it. But listen here.

161

I want you to think about an old fencerow with a rusty barbed-wire fence in it. I knowed you seen plenty of them."

"Sure I have."

"And haven't you seen a big oak tree with a piece of barbed wire running right through the middle of the trunk?"

"Course I have. Ever'body who's lived out in th' country has seen somethin' like that."

"Now," Carter says, "you tell me, how did that wire get in there?"

"Y' know as well as I do how it happened," Tucker says dismissively. "Whoever built th' fence decided t' nail th' wire t' th' tree when it was a young saplin', an' over time th' tree jes' growed up 'round it."

Carter nods. "Exactly. Now think about it, Tucker. Someone walked up to that young, tender sapling and, without any regard for what was right or wrong, took out a long, sharp steel steeple and hammered it deep into the tree to hold the wire in place. It probably tore the bark and splattered sap into the air. The tree didn't ask for it and certainly didn't deserve it to be done. If you think about it, it was a cruel thing to do to such a young thing."

Tucker's face and eyes redden.

"But that young sapling decided it wasn't going to be destroyed by its wounds. It decided to prove it was bigger than the person who harmed it. It accepted the hurt, embraced the experience, and grew around it. That, Tucker, is what forgiveness is."

Tucker's mouth is firmly set, but her chin is trembling. There is fear in her eyes.

Carter eases his hand across the tabletop. In a gentle tone, he says, "Give me your hand, old woman."

Tucker places her hand in his.

Carter squeezes it. "You can do this, Tucker. You can."

Tucker leans forward. "So how do y' do it? I don't think I even know how t' start."

"It's a day-by-day kind of thing," Carter answers. "You just try each day to let go of your bitterness and anger toward that person. Some days you'll do pretty good, and some days you'll think you're not getting anywhere. But you got to try every day."

He hesitates. "I know you don't talk to God 'cause you got questions about all that. I understand. But it wasn't until I started praying to God to help me forgive that I finally started feeling my heart change for the good."

Shaking her head, Tucker says, "I jes' don't know . . ."

"That's okay, Tucker. Give it time. Let what I've told you simmer for a few days. Now, I've got to be heading home. August will be there soon from basketball practice."

"How's he dealin' with Ella an' ever'thing?"

"He really doesn't say much. He seems to be throwing all his energy into playing basketball, so that's a good thing. What about April? How's she doing?"

"I ain't sure 'bout 'er. When she ain't in 'er room, she spends lots o' time cleanin' things. I seen 'er wash th' bathroom mirror five times, one right after th' other. She'll look in t' Ella's room, but she don't go in."

Later that night, after putting April to bed, Tucker goes to her own bedroom. She stands beside her bed and slowly lowers herself to her knees. Folding her hands, she lays them on the bed, then lowers her head.

"I ain't never done this b'fore. I don't know what I'm s'posed t' say 'r how I'm s'posed t' say it. Tell y' th' truth, I ain't fer sure made up m' mind 'bout y' yet. But Ella an' Carter put lots o' stock in y', so it can't hurt fer me t' try.

"I know this fer sure. If they's anybody on this earth that needs help, that needs savin', it's me. I've been mad an' angry a long, long time. An' I'm tired of it.

"I don't want t' fergive m' daddy, but it seems like that's where I gotta start. So I need y' t' help me.

"Well, that's all I got t' say right now. But I may be back later. Amen."

Later, the antique Seth Thomas mantle clock in Ella's living room strikes twice. The house is enveloped in darkness. The only sounds are the ones made by a tired house settling—a corner creaks, a floorboard pops.

The door to Ella's bedroom opens slowly. Barefoot and in her nightgown, April stands in the doorway. Looking at the bed, she sees Ella's face softly illuminated by the rays from the full moon shining through the window. On tiptoe, April approaches the bed.

The blue light of the moon gives Ella's face an ethereal glow. The sharp angles of her gaunt face cast geometric shadows.

April touches Ella's face as softly as a butterfly lighting upon a flower. Her hand travels down Ella's face to her neck, across her shoulder, and down the length of her arm. When she reaches Ella's hand, April envelops it with her fingers.

In barely a whisper, she says, "I love you, Grandmother. I love you. I don't want you to die. It makes my chest hurt when I think about living without you. I'm sorry I got upset and tore up my room and ruined my dolls. I won't ever do it again. I promise."

She stands there for a few moments, looking at her grandmother. Then she leans over and brushes her lips against Ella's cheek.

Turning, she tiptoes out the door and returns to her bed.

As April exits the bedroom, Ella reaches up and touches the place where April has kissed her. A smile passes across her face and a tear floats softly onto her pillow. She whispers, "Thank you, Lord."

CHAPTER THIRTY-FOUR

January 9

A t seven o'clock in the morning, as has become her routine, Tucker opens the door to Ella's room. She is surprised at seeing Ella sitting up in bed. "Well, lookee here! Somebody has finally woke up!" She strides to Ella's bedside and takes her hand. Tucker is struck by how bony it feels. "How y' feel this mornin'?"

Ella gives a weak smile. "How long have I been out of it?"

"'Bout four 'r five days. You'd sorta rouse up at times, but y' didn't make no sense. I did somethin' that'll prob'ly make y' mad, but I didn't know what else t' do an' Smiley Carter agreed with what I did. I called Doc Winston an' tol' 'im what was happenin'. He sent out 'is nurse, Martha, an' she put a catheter in. She showed me all 'bout it an' how to take care o' it. It'll keep y' from havin' t' git up an' go to th' bathroom."

Ella nods. "That's okay."

"Y' want me t' open th' curtains an' let some light in?"

"Sure, that would be nice. I'd like to be able to see outside."

Tucker goes to the window and ties the curtain back. Bright light fills the room. When Tucker turns back to Ella's bed, she almost stops in her tracks. Ella's color has become more green than yellow. The whites of her eyes look jaundiced. She looks emaciated. Resisting her urge to react to what she sees, Tucker sits on the side of Ella's bed and says, "Let me fix y' somethin' t' eat. What sounds good?"

"I think I'd like to try some hot tea and some chicken broth."

Standing up, Tucker says, "Sounds good. Be right back with it."

After a few minutes Tucker returns carrying a tray. She sets it on the bedside table and then pulls a straight-back chair close to the bed. She takes the cup off the tray and holds it up to Ella's lips.

Ella puts her hands around Tucker's to help guide the cup. She takes a couple of sips.

"That's a good girl," Tucker says quietly. She sets the cup on the tray. After spreading a napkin across Ella's chest, she picks up the bowl. Lifting a spoonful of the hot broth, she blows gently across it. Like a mama bird feeding her young, she carefully pours it into Ella's open mouth. Tucker watches Ella's larynx bob as she swallows.

Tucker continues to feed her until Ella holds up her hand.

"I'm full."

"Y' need t' be drinkin' whenever y' can. I'm sure you're dehydrated."

"I will when I can." She begins to try sliding down into her bed. "I want to lie down now."

Tucker assists Ella until she looks restful and then Tucker replaces the straight-back chair with the rocking chair.

"You know," Ella says, "I feel like I've been gone on a long trip . . . I don't know if I dreamed about my parents and grandparents . . . or if I actually met up with them on my trip . . . I think I remember seeing you sitting by my bed . . . but I could see me in the bed, too, . . . sort of like I was up above us looking down." She closes her eyes and falls silent.

Tucker waits for her to continue her story. When Ella doesn't speak for several moments, Tucker starts to get up.

Suddenly Ella starts speaking again with her eyes still closed. "I remember feeling like my parents wanted me to stay with them . . . and I felt torn on what to do . . . And, and an angel came to my side . . . I know it because its wings brushed against my face . . . It was as soft as . . . as a butterfly's wings . . ."

Ella eyes flutter open. She stares wide-eyed at the ceiling. "Oh, and then the most wonderful thing happened . . . I woke up in the middle of a dream . . . and April was here with me . . . really here, beside my bed . . . She told me she loved me . . . and she kissed me."

Ella's eyes close again.

Tucker frowns as she listens to Ella's ramblings, not sure if Ella believes they are true or that she imagined them. Tucker picks up the cup of tea. "I want y' t' take another sip 'r two o' this. Y' need fluids in y'."

Without protest, Ella allows Tucker to raise her head with one hand and put the cup to her lips with the other. She drinks two mouthfuls. "That's enough," she says. After Tucker lays her head back on the pillow, Ella says, "When Irvin gets here, I want both of you to come in here and wake me up, if I'm asleep. We need to plan my funeral."

At nine o'clock the sound of Smiley Carter's tractor can be heard as he pulls into Ella's front yard.

Tucker reaches into the kitchen cabinet and retrieves a coffee mug as Carter lets himself in the front door. She pours it full of coffee and offers it to him just as he enters the kitchen.

"Yes, yes," he says, "that's what I need. It's days like this that make me second-guess myself on if it was such a good idea not to have a pickup truck to drive sometimes. That wind cuts through you like a knife!"

DAVID JOHNSON

"Ever'body 'round thinks you're crazy anyway, Irvin, fer drivin' 'round on a tractor all th' time."

Carter freezes with his coffee cup halfway to his mouth. "What did you call me?"

Tucker smiles. "Irvin."

Carter rolls his eyes and shakes his head. "Oh my Lord, she done told you, didn't she?"

Still smiling, Tucker says, "Let's jes' say it sorta slipped out this mornin'."

"Now, you listen here, Tucker. That ain't nobody's business 'cept my family's. You just keep it to yourself, you hear?"

Tucker laughs. "Oh, calm down. I ain't gonna tell. I jes' think it's funny y' ain't never tol' what yore name is. B'sides, at least y' gotta first name."

"I don't have no idea why I ever told Ella what it was. But she took right up with it and has called me that ever since. I got to where it don't bother me for her to use it." He squints his eyes and frowns. "But I better not ever hear it out of your mouth."

Tucker waves dismissively at him. "Oh, drink yore coffee b'fore it gits cold. We got more important things t' talk 'bout. Ella been awake this mornin' an' took some nourishment."

"Praise Jesus!" Carter exclaims. "I just knowed she was going to bounce back!"

"Maybe so, but she wants us t' come in t' 'er room t'gether so we can plan 'er funeral."

Carter's happy expression remains frozen for an instant and then begins breaking into pieces like a window that's been struck by a stone. He sets his cup on the table. "Oh," he says quietly.

Tucker begins walking purposefully to Ella's room. "So, come on an' let's git this over with."

They find Ella fast asleep.

"She's asleep," Carter whispers. "We don't need to bother her."

168

"She tol' me t' wake 'er up if'n she was asleep." She walks over to Ella's bed. "Ella?" she says softly. When there is no response she touches Ella's shoulder. "Ella, it's Tucker."

Ella's eyes open but they are unfocused. "Tucker, is that you?"

"Right beside y'. Me an' Carter is here."

Ella turns to the sound of Tucker's voice. Clarity comes and she smiles. "Irvin."

Tucker backs up a few steps to allow Carter to step closer.

He bends down and carefully embraces Ella's dying body. Looking closely at her, he says, "Hello, sweet thing. Your old man is here."

Ella manages to smile. "Prop me up some. I can hardly breathe anymore when I'm lying flat."

Tucker puts her hand on Carter's arm. "Git back outta the way so I can fix 'er an' make 'er comfortable."

Carter starts to say something but changes his mind and gets out of Tucker's way.

She rolls a couple of pillows and situates them at Ella's shoulders and head. "How's that?"

"That's good. Thank you. So, you are both here . . . I want you to sit down . . . so we can talk."

Tucker motions Carter toward the straight-back chair and she sits in the rocker.

Her voice barely above a whisper, Ella says, "I think my time is very short . . . and I don't want to leave . . . without talking about . . . my funeral." She looks at Tucker. "Reach in the drawer of . . . this end table and . . . take out that folded piece . . . of yellow paper . . . Give it to Irvin to read."

Tucker silently obeys and hands the folded paper to Carter.

Carter opens it and begins reading to himself.

"Out loud," Ella says. "Read it out loud."

Carter clears his throat. "Number one: Do not notify any of my family of my death." Carter looks at Ella. "But your boy, Cade. Don't you want us to tell him? And what about your family in Mississippi?"

Pointing a bony finger at the paper, Ella says, "What it says is the way I want it to be."

"I done promised 'er," Tucker says, "that when th' end come, I'd do whatever she said. An' that's th' way it's gonna be." She looks at Carter. "You understand?"

Turning his attention back to the paper, Carter says, "Okay. Just as you say.

"Number two: The only people I want at my funeral are Tucker, Irvin Carter, August Tucker, April Tucker, and Shady Green. Besides them, the funeral director can be there and the preacher who did Maisy's funeral. I want him to do my funeral, too. That's number three.

"Number four: I want Tucker to wear a dress and shoes that I bought her for my funeral. You'll find them in my closet with her name on them."

In spite of her previous admonition to Carter, Tucker says, "Now wait jes' a minute—"

Ella holds up her hand to silence Tucker's protest. She points back at Carter and motions him to continue.

"Number five: I want Irvin to sing at my funeral." Carter's voice cracks. In a broken voice, he reads, "Any songs he wants to sing is okay with me." Carter swallows hard and wipes his tears.

His eyes widen as he looks at the next item on Ella's list of instructions. "And, number six is that I want to be cremated and my ashes scattered in Tucker's garden plot."

Tucker and Carter stare at Ella, their mouths agape.

CHAPTER THIRTY-FIVE

January 13

Tucker drapes the damp dish towel over the spout of the kitchen faucet. She scans the kitchen one more time to be sure she hasn't left anything from lunch out. Satisfied she is finished, Tucker heads toward the living room. Before she can sit down, someone knocks on the front door.

She opens the door to a tall, thin man with a receding hairline graying at the temples. His necktie is slightly askew. Part of a tattoo peeks out over his shirt collar. His oversized, silver belt buckle matches the metal-covered toes on his cowboy boots.

"Hello, Tucker," he says.

"Hello, Preacher," Tucker counters. "I'm glad y' come by. I guess y' done heared 'bout Miss Ella havin' cancer again. Looks like she ain't gonna be here long." She steps aside and says, "Come on in."

Preacher ducks to keep from hitting his head as he comes through the doorway.

Tucker sits on the end of the couch, leaving Preacher standing in the middle of the living room. "Well, ain't y' gonna sit down?"

At her prompting, he folds his lanky frame into an armchair.

"Ella just went t' sleep fer 'er afternoon nap, so I ain't gonna wake 'er up fer a bit. So y' jes' as well make yoreself comfortable."

Preacher frowns slightly. "Well, actually I'm not here to see Miss Ella." He reaches into his inside jacket pocket and brings out an envelope. "I'm here because of this."

Now it's Tucker's turn to frown. Looking cautious, she says, "What's in there? Y' don't know it, but we ain't had good luck 'round here when it comes t' letters an' such."

He opens the envelope and removes a letter. "I received this letter two months ago. It came from Ella. If you don't mind, I'd like to read it to you. It will help explain why I'm here."

Without waiting for Tucker to agree, he unfolds the letter and begins reading:

Dear Brother Sanders,

This is Ella McDade. I am Tucker's friend. I first met you at Maisy's funeral. Since then I've asked around about you and have found that you have an excellent reputation, a heart for people, and a heart for God. That you have preached for the Christian Chapel Church of Christ all these years draws me to you as well. I grew up in the Church of Christ but allowed life to get between me and God. However, I've made peace with God about that this week and feel confident I will be with him soon.

The reason I am writing you is because of my friend Tucker. She is the dearest thing to me on this earth. No one has loved me so purely and selflessly as she has. And I have tried my best to return her love in the same spirit. But because of the savage twists in life she has experienced, Tucker is all twisted up inside about God.

My request is that you spend time with her to help her see God, know God, and embrace God. You see, I want her to spend eternity with me in heaven.

In the next few months you will hear that I am dying of cancer. When you hear of this and suspect that my time is drawing near, please come.

If you do this for me, I will be eternally grateful.

Sincerely,

Ella McDade

Preacher refolds the letter, blows the envelope open, slides the letter in, and returns it to his pocket. Patting the pocket, he says, "That is the most unusual request I've ever received from a dying person. But, nonetheless, that is why I am here."

To hear Ella's words about her come from this man's lips has triggered a flood of emotions in Tucker. She feels as if she is drowning and struggles to catch her breath.

Preacher says, "I'm not interested in talking you into doing anything you don't want to do or making you believe something that you don't think is true. I just want to share with you what I know about God, though I'm still learning every day. So, why don't you tell me what your biggest stumbling block is in accepting God?"

Tucker finds herself suddenly calm. "That'll be easy." Pointing toward Ella's bedroom, she says, "Take that woman in there. There ain't a finer Christian woman walkin' this earth, an' yet she's sufferin' terrible. Why? An' what about me? When I was growin' up my daddy had his way with me anytime an' anywhere he wanted. An' me jes' a little girl! Why? If God is this lovin' bein' ever'body says he is, how can he let such awful things happen? What good does it do t' follow this God, if hellish things is still gonna happen to y'? Answer me that!"

Preacher doesn't flinch in the face of Tucker's barrage of accusations at his God. He allows Tucker's indictments to hang in the air until their own weight brings them one by one to the floor between them. He draws an easy breath, crosses his legs, and says, "The first thing I want to say to you is that I cannot explain everything about God. If I could, I would be him.

"But let me ask you this, have you ever heard of a man named Job?"

"Seems like I heared people talk 'bout someone havin' th' patience o' Job."

Preacher nods. "Yeah, I've heard the same thing, though I'm not sure I would describe him as patient. But he was a man who suffered maybe as much as anyone ever has and yet he still believed in and trusted God. He was a very wealthy, powerful man. But he lost his herd of thousands of livestock, his extra houses, all his children, and even his good health.

"Job's wife, like a lot of folks today, got angry about all that and told him to curse God. But you know what Job told her?"

Hanging onto his every word like a drowning person in a swollen stream grabs for every branch, Tucker shakes her head.

Preacher continues. "He said, 'Why shouldn't it have happened? Things don't happen because we deserve them, good or bad.'"

Tucker frowns and sits back. "What did he mean by that?"

"I think he meant that God never said life would be fair."

At this comment, Tucker springs forward to the edge of her seat again. "Really? That's what he said? Why, I've been sayin' that forever."

"Then you may have been closer to the truth than you thought and closer than a lot of people are. Bad things happen. Good things happen. It's just the way the world is, and there are volumes of books written to try and explain the why of it. But I'm not convinced we are even supposed to understand why. For me, the point is that God never said life would be a bed of roses. But he did promise us a bed of roses after we leave this earth, if we are true to him."

Tucker slowly eases back on the couch. "Well, I'll be. In all my days I ain't never heared it explained that way. It simplifies things fer me. An' I like simple."

They sit in silence for several minutes.

Tucker says, "Ella read t' me 'bout God bein' a shepherd an' 'bout 'im preparin' a place in heaven fer 'is sheep. After listenin' t' y' explain this other, I'd say this God is somebody I could follow. I know fer sure that if Ella's goin' t' heaven, I wanta be there with 'er. So, is there somethin' I gotta do?"

Preacher cocks his head. "Do? What do you mean?"

"Well, I 'member as a kid watchin' folks git baptized in th' Obion River on Sundays. Seemed like it was important t' 'em. An' it made ever'body happy who was standing on th' bank."

Preacher smiles. "Well, in my church we do baptize people. It shows they want to be God's children. It's how they are born again. And when they come out of the water, they are as sinless as newborn babies."

So intense is their conversation that neither of them has heard Smiley Carter drive up and walk onto the porch. When he opens the front door they both jump like they've been hit with an electric current.

"Well, what have we here?" Carter says.

Standing up and offering a handshake to Carter, Preacher says, "What we have here is someone who is ready to be baptized and become a child of the king!" He sweeps his free hand in Tucker's direction.

Carter's eyes pop open wide. Looking at Tucker, he says, "Is it true, Tucker?"

Tucker smiles. "It is."

"Praise Jesus!" Carter exclaims loudly.

"Shhh! Y' fool! Y' gonna wake Ella!"

All three hold their breath. Just when it seems everything is okay, a soft cry comes from Ella's room.

Tucker slaps Carter's arm. "I tole y', y' loudmouth bull!"

Carter follows close on Tucker's heels as she heads to the bedroom. When he looks back and notices that Preacher is standing in the living room, he motions for him to follow, too.

Once in the bedroom Carter is beside himself with excitement. "Ella," he says in breathless tones, "you ain't never gonna believe it! You ain't never gonna believe it! Tucker is going to be baptized!"

Ella's chest rattles when she gasps. Looking at Tucker she whispers, "Really?"

Tucker gets on her knees beside the bed and takes Ella's hand. "It's true m' dear friend. An' I'm excited. Excited I'll git t' see y' again one day."

"So," Preacher says, "where are we gonna do this baptizing?"

Everyone exchanges a puzzled look.

"A watering trough would work," Carter says, "but you'd catch pneumonia."

"An' I ain't 'bout t' set foot in th' Obion River."

"I guess I'll have to drive you to a church in town that has a heated baptistery," Preacher says. "The one at my country church will be as cold as a pond."

Tucker notices Ella pointing. "What, Ella? What do y' want?" She follows the line of sight of Ella's pointing finger. "Th' wall? What 'bout that wall?"

Ella stabs the air again.

Tucker looks at Carter. "What does she want?"

Carter scratches his head. "I'm not sure. On the other side of that wall is the bathroom and—Of course! That's it! She wants us to use her oversized claw-foot bathtub to baptize you in." Looking at Ella, he says, "Is that it?"

Ella smiles and manages to nod her head.

Preacher smiles and starts taking off his jacket and rolling up his sleeves. "Show me where it is, and I'll start drawing the water."

Carter escorts Preacher to the bathroom, and soon water can be heard running.

Tucker looks at Ella. "What am I s'posed t' wear? Jes' m' regular clothes like I got on?"

Ella takes a ragged breath and says, "In the closet . . . your dress."

"Y' mean m' funeral dress?"

Ella nods. "It's the funeral of . . . the old Tucker . . . and birth of . . . the new Tucker."

After several minutes Carter and Preacher come back to the bedroom. Carter freezes in the doorway. He rubs his eyes and shakes his head. "Tucker?"

Standing in the middle of the room, Tucker is turning slowly in front of a full-length mirror. To no one in particular, she says, "Ain't this th' prettiest shade o' purple y' ever saw? When I was a little girl purple was m' favorite color." She stops turning and looks at Carter. "It's what Ella wanted me t' wear fer m' baptizin'."

"I think," Carter begins, and then stops. "No, I *know* that is the prettiest purple dress I ever seen and you look majestic in it."

"Purple is the color for royalty in the Bible," Preacher adds admiringly. "If you're ready, the water is ready."

There is hesitation in Tucker and Carter. They look at each other and then at Ella.

"I want Ella t' see it," Tucker says.

"Yes," Carter agrees. "I was just thinking the same thing." He walks over to her bed and pulls the covers back. Carefully sliding one arm under her legs and the other under her shoulders, he lifts her as if she were a small child. Ella lays her head against his chest as she grimaces in pain.

In the bathroom Preacher says, "Tucker, I want you to step into the tub and stand there."

Holding his hand for balance, Tucker steps into the water.

"Now, Tucker, I want you to tell us what you are about to do and why you want to do it."

With her chin quivering, Tucker says, "I'm bein' baptized t' git rid o' th' ol' Tucker. I want 'er buried an' done away with. I want all th' bad things I done t' not haunt me no more. But most 'specially I want t' do this so someday I can join Ella in heaven."

All the time she is speaking, Carter is saying in muted tones, "Amen . . . yes, Lord . . . that's right . . . you tell it . . ."

When Tucker finishes speaking, Preacher says, "All's been said that needs to be said. It's time to bury the old and give birth to the new. I want you to ease yourself down into the tub now. Go ahead and lay yourself down. I'm going to push down a little so you will go under the water."

Tucker's face submerges and is distorted by the swirls of water. Then Preacher begins helping her to sit up and then stand again. The echo of the water dripping off her dress fills the quiet room.

Then a smile begins slowly at the corners of Tucker's mouth and spreads across her face. It is a big, broad smile. Her eyes dance with joy. And she begins to cry.

"Look at that water," Carter says, nodding toward the tub. "Ain't that the nastiest water you ever saw?"

Puzzled, Preacher looks at him and says, "What?"

"Look," Carter says, "can't you see the hate, the anger, the resentment, and the shame in there? It's all washed away. Pull the plug, Preacher, and send it all to hell."

"Yes, sir!" And with a flourish, Preacher lifts the tub's stopper.

CHAPTER THIRTY-SIX

January 16

Smiley Carter and August come through the front door of Ella's house shaking the snow off their coats and hats. Carter sets a suitcase by the door.

Speaking in a loud whisper, August says, "Man, I'm freezing! I can't feel my nose or fingers!"

Carter answers in his own whisper, "I know what you mean. I'm beginning to think I may be getting too old to drive a tractor in wintertime. A pickup truck is sounding more and more tempting."

"I've been telling you, you need to get one. I need to learn how to drive a vehicle that's not used for plowing. All my friends are driving."

"That don't mean nothing to me. If all your friends jumped off a cliff, would you jump off, too?"

August rolls his eyes as he peels off his coat.

Tucker comes into the living room from Ella's bedroom. "Hey there, you two," she whispers. "Come on into th' kitchen so I can git y' some coffee 'r hot chocolate."

When they walk into the kitchen they see April spraying Windex on the counters and wiping them off. She turns at the sound of their footsteps.

"Hello, April," Carter says quietly.

Smiling, August says, "Hey there, Sis."

April stares at them for a second, then turns around and sprays the counter again and rubs it vigorously.

When Carter and August look at Tucker, she shrugs her shoulders.

"They's coffee made on th' stove. I'll boil some water fer hot chocolate."

Carter helps himself to the coffee and cradles the warm mug in his cold hands. He takes a sip of the steaming liquid. "Ahhh, I can feel it go all the way down to my toes. Feels good."

"I see y' brought yore things with y'," Tucker says. "I think it best that ya'll just stay here fer th' next little bit. I jes' don't think she's gonna be here much longer."

April stops in the middle of her cleaning and stands like a statue.

"How's her breathing?" Carter asks.

"I can tell it's gittin' harder fer 'er t' git a breath. I keep 'er propped up in bed all th' time now. Seems like it helps."

"Is she awake any?"

"At times she is sort o' alert. Most o' th' time, though, she jes' lies there."

April sprays the same counter again and tears off fresh paper towels to wipe it with.

Carter looks at August. "Tell Tucker what you want to do."

Tucker raises her eyebrows. "What's this?"

August looks at his feet. "I had this writing assignment in school and I decided to write it about Miss Ella." Looking up at his grandmother, he says, "I want to read it to her before she dies."

April turns around so that she is facing everyone.

Tucker steps over to August and embraces him. "Oh my Lord, ain't that th' nicest thing. Well, I'll guarantee she'll want t' hear it an' that she'll like it."

"It's not all that good," August says, "but I still want to read it to her."

"Hush your mouth," Carter scolds. "It's straight from the heart and speak eloquently of what Ella has meant to you and to us. That's what important. Anything that comes straight from the heart is beautiful."

"Yore pa's right," Tucker agrees. "An' Ella's all 'bout th' heart."

Suddenly, April says, "Me, too."

Everyone spins in her direction.

"What did you say?" Tucker asks.

"Me, too," April repeats.

"You, too, what?" August asks.

Setting the bottle of Windex and damp paper towels on the counter, she walks out of the kitchen and disappears into her bedroom.

They all exchange questioning glances.

In a moment April returns with a paper in her hand. She carries it to Tucker and hands it to her.

Tucker inspects it. "You drawed 'er a picture, didn't y'?"

April nods her head.

Tucker gets to one knee so that she is eye level with April. "Tell me 'bout yore picture."

"Those are angels." April points as she describes her drawing. "And that's Jesus in heaven. And that's Grandmother in the bed."

Tucker turns the picture so that the others can see it.

"That's a cool picture," August says.

"And them angels," Carter says, "have they come to take Ella to heaven?"

April nods.

"That's what I thought. Child, that's one beautiful picture. It makes me smile. And, like your brother's poem, it's straight from the heart. Yes, sir, it's beautiful."

Tucker looks at the drawing again. "Ella's smiling in yore picture. That's nice."

"She's smiling," April says, "because she sees the angels."

Carter blows his nose loudly into his bandanna. "Ain't these two some of the best children alive? I know they is."

"Why don't I go see if'n Ella's up t' us comin' t' see 'er." Tucker makes her way to Ella's room. The setting sun has left the room dark since Tucker was last in. Tucker tiptoes to the bed and turns on a small lamp on the bedside table.

Ella is not moving.

Tucker looks at her for several moments.

Then suddenly Ella gasps for a breath. Her chest rattles. She expels the breath as violently as she has taken it in and then falls still and silent.

"Ella?" Tucker says softly. "Ella, yore family wants t' come in 'n see y'."

Ella's eyes flutter open. She turns her head toward Tucker's voice. "Did you say 'my family'?"

"Yes. August and April 'specially want t' see y'. They brung somethin' fer y'."

Ella makes an effort to become more alert. "Please, bring them in."

Tucker exits the room and returns with everyone in single file behind her.

Tucker stands at the foot of the bed and says, "Y' kids step on up so's she can see an' hear y'."

The children cautiously approach Ella's bed.

"April, y' go first an' show 'er yore picture y' drawed."

April brings out the picture she has been holding behind her back and holds it up in front of Ella.

"How pretty," Ella says.

"It's a picture of you," April explains. "It's what it will look like when the angels come to get you and take you to Jesus in heaven. You're going to be smiling and be all pretty again."

Ella clutches the picture to her chest and closes her eyes. Opening them, she looks at April and says, "You are exactly right . . . but remember . . . you've been my angel . . . here on earth . . . and some-day . . . we'll be together . . . again."

Ignoring her own tear-streaked face, Tucker says, "Now y', August."

August reaches inside his jeans and takes out a folded piece of paper. Unfolding it, he says, "This is something I wrote for an assignment in English. It's about you and I wanted to read it to you." He clears his throat and begins reading:

AN UNEXPECTED FROST
by
August Tucker

I have counted the cost
Of an unexpected frost.
It is measured by what is lost
From what was gained.

If the greater the gain
the greater the loss is true,
then my loss will be measured by the empty feeling in my heart
when with this world you are through.

I have no regrets
for the loss I will feel
after you leave us here.

I only wish you had come sooner
Because you taught us how to heal.

I wish you well on your flight to heaven from here.
I hope to see you again when before the throne I, too, will kneel.

CHAPTER THIRTY-SEVEN

January 17

Candlelight fills Ella's bedroom with soft amber light. Dark shadows that refuse to be chased away by the flames bob and weave against the walls and ceiling like boxers in a ring. The smell of lavender fills the room.

Carter sits in the straight-back chair. Sleep keeps pulling his head down toward his chest. But he jerks himself awake; his head acts like the bobbing float on a fishing line.

Tucker sits in the rocking chair, attentive to the sounds of Ella's breathing. More than once she has gotten out of her chair, believing Ella has died, such a long time having passed between breaths. But then Ella's chest would heave and she would draw another ragged breath.

Tucker gets up and goes to the kitchen, returning in a moment with two cups of coffee. Tapping Carter's chair with her foot, she says, "Here, this'll help."

Carter startles awake and stands up. He stretches his arms over his head and then rubs his face. "Did I go to sleep? Is there any change?"

"Y' dozed a bit. Ain't been no change in th' last twenty-four hours."

They drink their coffee in silence.

When she finishes, Tucker gets in bed beside Ella. She rests Ella's head against her breast and holds her there with her arm. She slowly rocks from side to side while she strokes Ella's drawn face.

Ella's eyes are open but not seeing. Her mouth is open, too.

As if she were talking to a baby, Tucker says, "It's okay, honey. It's okay t' let go. We's all done said our good-byes. There ain't nothin' left t' say, 'cept we'll see y' on th' other side."

Ella snatches a breath out of the air.

Tucker looks at Carter standing at the foot of the bed. "How come she don't go? What's keepin' 'er here?"

Carter wipes his face with his damp bandanna. "It's hard to say. Maybe she got to the edge of the River Jordan and got scared all of a sudden. Maybe she's waiting for the angels or somebody to escort her across."

"Can y' pray 'bout it? Would it be okay fer y' t' pray she go on?"

"I don't see why not. She's God's child and seems ready to go." Grasping a bedpost, Carter goes down on one knee and lifts his face toward the ceiling. "Mighty God above, it seems it's time for you to receive one of your saints. She's been suffering so much the last few days, Lord. It don't seem fair. Please, if it be your will, cut the silver thread that has her spirit tethered to her body and give her wings to fly with the angels to your bosom. In the name of sweet Jesus I offer this prayer. Amen."

When Carter finishes, the high-pitched strains of Tucker's voice suddenly fill the room as she sings:

Amazing grace! How sweet the sound!
That saved a wretch like me!
I once was lost, but now I'm found;

Was blind, but now I see.

'Twas grace that taught my heart to fear,
And grace my fears relieved.
How precious did that grace appear
The hour I first believed!

Working to keep his composure, Carter joins with Tucker:

Through many dangers, toils, and snares,
I have already come.
'Tis grace hath brought me safe thus far,
And grace will lead me home.

August and April come into the room, stand on each side of Carter, and join in singing with them:

When we've been there ten thousand years,
Bright shining as the sun,
We've no less days to sing God's praise
Than when we first begun.

Just as music had filled it, the room is now filled with silence. Carter, August, and April look at Tucker and Ella.

Tucker looks down at her friend.

Ella's mouth is closed in a smile and her eyes are closed, as if in sleep.

Tucker bends her ear down to Ella's nose and mouth. After a full two minutes passes, she looks up, smiles, and says, "She's on 'er way t' that better place."

EPILOGUE

January 23

Tucker walks through the empty rooms of her house, arriving back in the living room where April is sitting on a bedsheet that has been tied up with all of their clothes inside. Tucker looks out the window and sees the sheriff's patrol car approaching her house.

"They's comin'," she says to April.

As the patrol car gets to the front of the house, a black sedan slowly approaches from the opposite direction. Sheriff Ron Harris takes note of the car but thinks nothing of it. He turns off into Tucker's front yard. In his rearview mirror he sees that the black sedan is pulling in behind him.

He shifts the patrol car into park and picks up his Stetson hat. Speaking to Deputy King in the passenger seat, he says, "Now, I'm only going to say this once. You do not get out of this car unless you hear me call your name. Is that understood?"

"Yes, sir. I got it, sir. No problem."

Harris gets out of his car just as the driver of the black sedan opens his door. Out steps a very short man. He is dressed in a black pin-striped suit, complete with vest and a chain hanging from a pocket watch. His white handlebar mustache dwarfs him. On top of his head is a black derby hat.

The man nods at the sheriff and proceeds toward Tucker's front door, briefcase at his side.

"Just a minute," Harris says.

The man stops and turns to face the sheriff towering over him. Speaking in a fast clip, he says, "J. P. Worthington, the third, of the law firm Worthington, Blythe, Epstein, and O'Keefe at your service." He offers his hand toward the sheriff.

Harris shakes his hand politely. "Are you lost, mister?"

"That," he answers indignantly, "would be highly unlikely as I've never been lost in my life. I have a keen sense of direction. It's the blamedest thing. Don't know how I got it, but surely I was born with it. No, sir, I'm not lost. I'm here to see Miss Tucker."

Harris pushes his hat back a bit and studies the man. "Well, it just so happens that so am I."

"Delightful! Then why don't we proceed together?" Without waiting for a reply from Harris, Worthington strides purposefully toward the porch, climbs the steps, and knocks on the door.

Tucker opens the door and stares down at the incongruent figure on her porch.

"Are you Miss Tucker?" he asks.

Keeping her eye on the sheriff climbing the steps, Tucker answers. "I'm jes' Tucker," she says suspiciously. "No 'Miss.'"

"Well, Miss Tucker, my name is J. P. Worthington, the third, of the law firm of Worthington, Blythe, Epstein, and O'Keefe. And I am here with a matter of the utmost importance."

"Well, sir, Mr. . . ."

"Folks call me J. P."

"Mr. J. P., the sheriff is also come t' see me." Casting her eyes toward Harris, she says sarcastically, "Seems like this day I'm suddenly quite popular."

"Oh, I see," J. P. says. "Well, my business won't take but just a few minutes, then I'll be on my way and the sheriff can tend to whatever business he has with you." Giving room for discussion, he squats down, opens his briefcase, and lifts out a sheaf of papers.

He reaches in his pocket and removes a pair of glasses. After he scans the document to refresh his memory, he says, "Yes, yes, I remember now. Miss Tucker, I believe you were acquainted with the late Mrs. Ella McDade."

Tucker gives the sheriff a puzzled expression. He responds by shrugging his shoulders.

She folds her arms across her chest and says, "Sure, I knowed Miss Ella. What about it?"

"Well, Miss Tucker, it seems that when Mrs. McDade was married to Mr. McDade, he encouraged her to take out a life insurance policy on herself. That he encouraged her to do it rather than doing it himself is what makes this situation all the more fascinating." A tinge of excitement is in his voice; he relishes the telling.

When Tucker's face doesn't reflect his excitement, he says, "Don't you see? Of course the beneficiary to the policy was Mr. McDade when she first took it out. But because she was the one who took out the policy, she was free to change the beneficiary whenever she wanted to whomever she wanted."

"Well, I'll be," the sheriff says behind J. P.

J. P. turns, pleased that someone sees where this is going. "You see, don't you? Isn't it a sweet twist? I just love these kinds of stories."

He bends down and takes another paper out of his briefcase. He hands it toward Tucker. "Miss Tucker, I am very pleased. No, I am delighted to present to you this cashier's check in the amount of $250,000.00."

Tucker's eyes blink rapidly.

Sheriff Harris whistles loudly. "Oh my Lord!"

"Y' mean?" Tucker begins slowly. "Y' mean all that money is mine? An' I can do with it what I want?"

J. P. beams. "Yes, you may, Miss Tucker." Suddenly he remembers something. "Oh, yes, there was one more thing." He bends down and shuffles through his briefcase, muttering to himself. "Here it is!" he exclaims. "It's a letter from Mrs. McDade that she wanted read to you when the check was delivered."

Harris sees Tucker's knees almost buckle. He rushes to her side. "Easy, Tucker. I know this is quite a shock. Let me get you a chair from the kitchen." He hurries to the kitchen and returns with a chair. "Here, sit down."

Tucker sits down slowly, her mind reeling.

J. P. unfolds the letter and begins reading:

Hello, Tucker.

Since this letter is being read to you, it means I'm in that better place you and I have talked about so many times. Please don't grieve for me, for I am at peace. This present that you are being given today seemed the best way that I could help you with your life after I left. Money is certainly not everything. You showed me that. But it can be helpful if it is used wisely.

I encourage you to put your trust in Mr. Worthington's advice in all matters financial. He is a good man and will serve your best interests.

Now, you can save your farm or you can sell it and buy anything else you want. But I hope you will at least keep your garden plot. I want to be there with you in February when you plant your potatoes and in March when you plant your early corn. I'll be feeling your drops of sweat when you pick beans in July and I'll be jealous that I can't eat a mess of your greens in the fall.

One more thing. Why don't you surprise Irvin and buy him a pickup truck?

ACKNOWLEDGMENTS

I have many people who deserve a bow of thanks for helping me bring Tucker's story to the world.

I want to thank the hundreds of coworkers at McKenzie Medical Center, people that I see on a daily basis, for giving me constant words of encouragement to keep writing Tucker's story. Seeing their enthusiasm and love for Tucker and her family certainly spurred me on to continue the saga. You guys are the best! But most importantly, all thanks to God who has blessed me far beyond measure, giving me talents I didn't know I had until I stumbled upon them.

ABOUT THE AUTHOR

David Johnson has worked in the helping professions for over thirty-five years. He is a licensed marriage and family therapist with a master's degree in social work and over a decade of experience as a minister. In addition to the four novels comprising the Tucker series, he has authored several nonfiction books, including *Navigating the Passages of Marriage* and *Real People, Real Problems* and has published numerous articles in national and local media. David also maintains an active blog at www.thefrontwindow.wordpress.com. When he's not writing, he is likely making music as the conductor of the David Johnson Chorus.